Tomassini's Trophy
William Daye

WilliamEmersonBooks—Greensboro, NC
ISBN: 979-8-218-00623-5
Library of Congress Control Number: 2022909011
Title: Tomassini's Trophy
Author: William Daye
Digital distribution | 2022
Paperback | 2022

Cover designed by GetCovers

Dedication

This book is dedicated to Walter A. Edwards, who passed away on February 26th, 2022.

John C. Maxwell once said, "teamwork makes the dream work, but a vision becomes a nightmare when the leader has a big dream and a bad team." When I decided to republish Tomassini's Trophy, I wasn't sure how the process would turn out. It exceeded my expectations, and I couldn't have dreamt that the story would've taken such a positive turn. I want to thank the following people on my Fiverr team for their help and tireless efforts in making this book the best it could be.

Garret Lee
J Flowers-Olnowich
Ahmed Muzammil
Isabella Warner
Ana Hantt
Josie Baron
Daniel
S.D. Johnson
Simona

Chapter One
Adolescent All-Star

Alex Tomassini wasn't just the best soccer player at Beaumont Christian School—his fame bordered on a celebrity. Only days away from starting eighth grade, teachers concluded that Alex was one of their brightest and most hardworking students. The middle son of a United States senator, Alex could've ruled the hallways at school with snobbery and the undeserving sense of entitlement expected of kids from elite families. But that's just not who Alex was. The only thing he cared about more than grades and soccer was his standing within his family. He would not tarnish their name.

Being underestimated by his family and others irritated Alex his entire life. As he received a pass from Ram goalkeeper Egan off his thigh outside his team's penalty box, Alex wondered how to escape from the enormous shadow of his older brother S.J. He turned and flashed across the center mark of Allerton Academy's soccer field. Lunging into Falcon territory and eyeing teammates trying to break away from defenders, Alex weighed his next maneuver. Agile at five feet and six inches, he had a successful attacking midfielder's field vision and speed. *Come on, guys*, he thought, hearing the labored breathing of opponents nearby. *Can somebody get open?*

He gritted his teeth as a defender slammed into him. It was mid-afternoon on a Thursday in late August, temperatures inching past ninety-five, and he was not enjoying it. But these temperatures weren't anything new to Alex, who understood the scorching heat was well above average for Greenbriar, Connecticut. Noticing his body and his teammates soaked in sweat reminded him how intense today's matchup was.

"Hey, Alex!" Phil called out a short distance away. "Pass to the left, man."

Phil was about the same height but much skinnier and more flexible than others. He had wavy light brown hair and beady ocean-blue eyes. Since meeting at a daycare center, Alex's best friend, Phil, had a strong loyalty to his childhood buddy, and the two were inseparable

When Alex heard this, he knew Phil had shaken his defender. He couldn't get the ball from where he was to where it needed to be without taking a risk. He leaned his body left, then stepped over the ball with his right foot, which resulted in his opponent opening his legs just enough. At that exact moment, he clipped the ball with the outside of his right foot and performed a classic nutmeg right into the spot Phil should've been.

It came at a cost, though. Alex tried to get around his defender but got tripped up by his opponent's foot and tumbled over. He landed hard but managed to look up from his stomach to see the ball arrive precisely where his teammate needed it. Alex couldn't help but sport a grin in satisfaction. Throwing a quick thumbs-up in the coach's direction, he sprang back up.

Alex enjoyed playing soccer with his friends. He loved how everyone in school looked up to him and admired his many talents. A few days earlier, while stuffing workout gear in his duffel bag in his bedroom, he smiled at the photos on his bedroom dresser of him holding trophies with his teammates with a soccer goal behind them. Alex couldn't wait to have that experience again.

There's nothing better than being on a winning team when you're the hero.

Alex knew he was the best. It didn't matter how many coaches and people around Greenbriar doubted him. He recognized that he'd have to play better than ever this season to lead the Rams to a championship, but that only fueled his fire more. *In the end*, Alex thought, imagining a professional soccer stadium,

I'll show everyone-- even Dad, that I'm just as great as S.J.

Alex dashed around Allerton Academy territory with an opponent matching him stride for stride on the field. "Let's go, boys!"

I want to be more than S.J.'s little brother. Everybody reminds me of how much better he's always been. Will I ever be good enough? I wish Dad showed as much interest in my games as he did in my older brother.

The deepest desires and thoughts haunted Alex as he studied Phil tracking the ball off his cleat mid-stride along the left touchline. Alex cringed as a Falcon centerback collided with his teammate and sent the ball bouncing away out of the corner of his eye.

The Falcon goalie sprang forward and grabbed the loose ball. Alex tracked the ball as it sailed to the center circle. A pair of Allerton Academy players with a lone Beaumont Christian player, Connor, jostled as they battled for possession.

"You've got this, Connor." Alex settled himself just outside the center circle. "Head it over here."

The ball bounced off the boys' head before Alex trapped it between his legs and dribbled past a pair of defenders; before pulling the ball back. He lifted his leg and swung his right cleat. It spun toward the goal and ripped through the air before the Falcon goalie deflected the ball out of play.

The whistle blew as Alex shook his head.

"Nice try, Al," said Nick, a taller forward with buzzed black hair and chocolate-chip-brown eyes, whose voice was deeper than the others. "I thought you had that."

"Ditto," Alex interlocked his fingers around his head to catch his breath while trotting beside Nick to the Ram bench. "You know how seriously I take our shooting drills."

"Almost as much as you do warmups," Phil said as he curled an arm around Alex's shoulder. "Very."

"Sorry, dude." Alex used his already moist jersey to wipe his sweaty forehead. "I always play my hardest."

"Darn straight, Tomassini." Kellen jogged up beside his teammate and patted Alex on the back. He was the Ram's top defender and happened to be the coach's son, the spitting image of his dad.

Allerton is playing hard today.

Alex leaned over and touched the front of his cleats. Grimacing at the tightness in his legs as he returned to a standing position, he realized how intense their game was.

The Falcons weren't this good last season.

Alex snatched a giant orange sports bottle from the student manager. Scanning the away side bleachers, he spotted his mom and older brother sitting in the middle top row. Clarisse Tomassini smiled and waved. Seventeen-year-old Salvatore Tomassini JR., better known as S.J., played varsity soccer for Donnington Prep high school and was considered the best player in the state, leaned back, intrigued by what he'd seen on the field.

I can't believe Dad is missing the game for golf with his donors.

"Way to hustle, boys!" Coach Schallhorn's voice carried. Sweeping his large brown eyes over the fifteen players, he raised an eyebrow. "Everybody's gotten it done on both sides of the pitch. The defense is shutting down everything Allerton brings; don't let up; midfielders keep up the pressure and support on defense. Although I'm pleased with our forwards and offense overall, you must play better. Egan, you've had some exceptional saves on goal. Keep bringing it."

Coach Schallhorn who towered over most of the boys, had a bulky stature that resembled a hummer. The muscles in his arms and legs protruded from the crisp blue polo and khaki shorts he wore. His dark brown hair, high and tight, served as a reminder of his time spent in the marines. Alex couldn't help but swallow a lump in his throat. As an authoritarian coach, Mr. Schallhorn dictated everything for the team, including workouts, training sessions, and game plans. Coach Schallhorn expected compliance from all Ram players.

"We've got a corner following the timeout. Four of you are in Allerton Academy's penalty box, one of you stays near the goalpost, and another will be outside the penalty box to run and take the shot. Alex, as the corner taker, you've got to make smart decisions and set your teammates up."

The whistle blew.

"Alright, boys." Coach Schallhorn's gaze bounced between the field and Ram players. "Hustle out there and make something happen. Rams on three; one-two-three!"

"Rams!" The boys in royal blue with gold trim raised their arms in unison and then broke their huddle.

"Go Rams, go!" the Beaumont Christian fans shouted on their feet and pumped their fists in the air. "Go Rams, go!"

The Rams retreated onto the field and set up their corner kick as the Falcons lined up defensively.

Alex gave Connor, the Ram right wing, a once-over. He studied how his teammate raised his knee toward his chest outside Allerton Academy's penalty box and winced. Although he remembered his buddy grew two inches over the summer and appeared fit as ever, Alex wondered if Connor was tired or if something else was at play entirely

Hope Connor can last the season, Alex thought. *He almost quit last year.*

"Hey, Connor." Alex swatted his teammate on the arm. "You good?"

"Obviously," Connor scoffed. "If I weren't, I'd be on the sidelines with Vance."

"Geez." Alex frowned. "You want some cheese with that wine?"

"Can it." Connor gave Alex a stink-eye. "Just leave me alone!"

Alex shook his head at his friend's reaction. He stole a quick look at the scoreboard, revealing a tied score of zero with less than thirty seconds to play. As he observed his teammates set up around the Falcon penalty box marked by defenders, Alex tried determining who might get open first.

The whistle blew.

Alex backpedaled three steps, aimed his kick, sprinted up to the corner flag post, and booted the ball into a sea of dark blue and white jerseys. He eyed Phil flashing to where the pass would be before lifting his knee. Studying his best friend push off the ground with his right leg and strike the ball, Alex's heartbeat doubled in speed.

"Yeah, Phil." Alex raced around Allerton Academy's penalty box. "You've got it, bud."

I had your brother S.J. in class. Everything seemed to come naturally. You've got to work harder if you expect to surpass your brother. S.J. is the best soccer player to graduate from Beaumont Christian in a long time. You've got a lot to live up to, Alex.

Alex recalled all the things teachers and Coach Schallhorn said to him. He heard the Beaumont Christian fans shout a collective "ooh" as the ball hit the goal post's top and bounced off.

"Who's got the ball on the right?" Coach Schallhorn called from the left touchline. "You'd better not let the Falcons get past the halfway line, Connor!"

Allerton isn't going anywhere.

Alex hustled near the center circle and followed his marked man. He glanced at how Connor trailed behind a Falcon midfielder who almost resembled a car with a flat tire, then frowned. Widening his eyes at the sight of his teammate and opponent's legs becoming tangled up just after the Allerton Academy player lofted a pass in his direction, Alex grew concerned for Connor.

Alex saw the ball coming toward him within seconds and puffed his chest out. He stepped in front of Falcon star Braylon Gonzalez, gathered the ball in, and let it fall to his feet. While faking right and slashing left, Alex felt a sharp pain emerge in the back of his right leg.

"Over here, dude," Phil waved his arm. "I got this!"

Alex fired a bullet pass in his best friend's direction, ignoring the pain. He hobbled around and paid attention to the action. Considering he'd hustled across the field all afternoon without subbing out, Alex figured it was a tweak and no big deal.

"Do your thing, buddy," Alex smiled.

Alex's heart pounded as Phil collected the ball and then feinted past a defender. He knew as much as he wanted the ball in his possession, his best friend gave their team the best chance to win. Tipping his chin in the air when Phil lifted his leg and sent a shot off just outside Allerton Academy's penalty box, Alex realized the shot was money.

The ball rotated near Allerton Academy's goal. The Falcon goalie saw the shot approaching and sprinted right. As he stretched his arms and dove toward the incoming white sphere, the Falcon goalie secured the ball with both hands and crawled to his feet.

The scoreboard remained 0-0.

The whistle blew for the end of regulation as Alex hurtled toward Phil and draped an arm around his shoulder.

"Nice try, Pal," Alex shook his teammate lightly. "You'll get the next one."

##

Clontz's café was a small but lively restaurant within a few miles of Beaumont Christian School in a busy shopping center. It was a popular spot for locals and visitors seeking a homey atmosphere with a diverse menu. Sports teams of all types surged there, with athletes and parents alike for post-game meals. The café was open seven days a week and only closed on Christmas, New Years, and Thanksgiving.

"Yo Al," Nick gulped some iced water. "Did you get your schedule yet?"

"Yeah," Alex shoveled part of his tuna sandwich. "Bible class with Bettencourt, Earth Science with Conway, Algebra 1 with Schallhorn, Social Studies with Gentry, and Farnsworth's Language Arts, just to name a few."

"We've got a few together," Phil said, swigging a strawberry banana smoothie. "I wish we were in the same Bible one, though."

"Why?" Connor sneered at his teammate. "Studying the Bible is a waste of time."

The four sat in their usual booth enjoying post-game snacks and chatted over their school schedules. Phil settled next to Alex while Connor planted himself beside Nick.

The one thing Alex loved about attending a Christian School was the religion classes. He learned so much about living according to what the Bible teaches. While he understood that not everyone in their grade was as enthusiastic and accepting of God in their lives as him, Alex strived to live out the fruits of the Spirit.

He thought *I was pretty good at kindness, joy, goodness, and charity, but peace, patience, gentleness, self-control, and others needed work.*

"Since when?" Phil raised an eyebrow. "You always enjoyed studying the Bible together. We all did."

"Not anymore," Connor stole a potato chip from Alex's bag, "seeing as my family stopped going to church, I stopped caring."

"Darn, buddy." Alex frowned. "You know you're welcome to come with us anytime."

"Ditto," Nick smiled, draping an arm around his teammate's shoulders. "We've got your back."

Alex smiled at how supportive his pals were. Even though their families all attended different churches and held distinctive beliefs about religion, they stood by each other. While he considered themselves the fantastic four since they all attended Beaumont Christian for the last eight years, Alex knew they had secrets.

As the conversation shifted away from school schedules and religion to soccer season, Alex's mind remained stuck on Connor's family not going to church. He couldn't figure out if his buddy were more upset about that or if something else had happened. Although he wanted to find out more, Alex wasn't going to push Connor any further.

"I can't get over how difficult it was to beat Allerton," Alex finished off his tuna sandwich, "there was no need for overtime."

"I know," Phil chugged the rest of his smoothie, then set the glass down. "It's insane with how hard we played."

Nick drained his iced water. "Yup, we're lucky we competed against one of the weaker in the Pac-7."

"No kidding," Connor ran his fingers through his now-flattened dark brown fauxhawk, "and it'll only get more challenging."

Alex heard his pal's assessment of their recent game. Even though he knew his primary role as team captain was leading teammates to victory, Alex recognized there was something more significant than winning that he carried on his shoulders. In their times of need, being there for others forced him to question if he'd succeeded at either.

Even though we're 2-0, we've got to play better.

"True." Alex flexed his neck. "It's nothing we can't handle, though."

"No." Nick's gaze bounced between his three friends. "But we'll need to stay healthy and look out for one another, especially during tougher games."

"Like Greenbriar Day," Phil confirmed. "They're the best team in the conference."

"And have been for a while," Nick munched on an apple. "We haven't beaten them since Al's brother played."

Alex's mind drifted back to last year's conference championship game against Greenbriar Day. He'd dragged himself across the field and matched Spencer Donnelly, their rival star midfielder, stride for stride. While he still swore pure adrenaline allowed him to muster through the game's final minutes, Alex admitted God got him through that grueling matchup. Although he had to settle underneath his teammate's shoulders and be carried off the field, chills emerged on Alex's bare arms whenever he gave thought to those critical games on their schedule.

"Don't remind me," Alex exhaled. "I hear about it all the time on campus."

"No sweat, bro," Phil slapped his buddy's thigh. "This year will be different. We've got that new kid from New York, Landon something."

"Bettencourt," Nick drained his iced water. "He's shown out at workouts and training lately. He'll be a huge contributor."

Alex nodded in agreement. He knew the kid was incredible and would probably start by mid-season, if not sooner. While studying his pals, Alex noticed Connor crossed his arms and made a sour face.

"Huge contributor?" Connor scoffed. "I guess I don't play a part in the team's success."

"Shut up," Phil argued. "You know that's not true."

"Yeah," Nick turned to his teammate. "Schallhorn always says we win and lose as a team."

"That's bull," Connor shot back. "You know he hates me for not scoring more and stepping up on defense when it matters."

Alex looked away. He thought back to his interaction with his teammate earlier following a timeout. Even as he considered how Connor snapped when he'd checked on him, Alex knew something was going on.

"No worries," Alex offered an encouraging grin. "Everybody has an awful game."

"Yup," Nick nodded. "Don't beat yourself up."

"You don't understand," Connor's shoulders dropped. "It's not just an awful game. I haven't felt right since the season started."

"How so?" Alex gave Connor a doubtful look. "I thought you passed your physical and everything."

If Alex hadn't started putting the puzzle pieces of his teammate's anxiousness together yet, he would now. After returning from their Little League World Series run, he noticed that his buddy acted differently. While considering Connor was super exhausted as they all were, Alex sensed something was going on at home.

"I did," Connor sighed. "But it's got nothing to do with injuries."

"Then what?" Phil cracked his knuckles. "Something's on your mind."

"Right," Alex made eye contact with his buddy. "Whatever it is, we can help you with it."

"I've felt down lately," Connor softened his tone, "like things that used to be fun aren't anymore."

Alex pressed his lips together. He'd have those feelings after a terrible game or test. Even as normal as it was to second-guess himself and fixate on mistakes, Alex took comfort in knowing it'd eventually pass. Although this was true for him, it wasn't for Connor.

"You mean like soccer?" Alex scratched his head.

"Yes!" Connor rolled his head between his shoulders to ease tension. "It's felt like a chore to warm up, stretch, or even do drills."

"Darn," Nick shook his head. "Have you told anyone?"

"Only Egan," Connor admitted. "He's my closest friend and the one who's been by my side since everything started."

Alex wasn't sure what to say. He'd noticed recently how distracted and halfhearted his teammate was on the field. Even though Connor dropped hints that he was hurting but hadn't said anything definitive, it left Alex wishing he could help.

"I'm glad someone's helping," Nick smiled. "It's important to lift each other when we fall."

"Yup," Alex studied his teammate, crossing his arms over his chest, "and assist with carrying each other's burdens."

Alex heard the opening notes of Eminem's "Not Afraid" blare. He saw his friend fish the phone from his pocket and stare at the screen. As he surveyed Connor punching the screen with a finger and then rolling his eyes, Alex knew whoever was on the other end upset his pal.

"Yes!" Connor twisted his face in pain as he slid from the booth. "I'm coming, bye!"

"Is everything ok?" Alex checked out his teammate.

"Leave me alone!" Connor slammed a hand on the table. "It's none of your business."

At that moment, Connor muttered something under his breath and stormed away toward the café entrance as

Alex's stomach tightened in knots. He wondered what his pals were thinking. With the team surviving their first few games by slim margins and teammates bickering at each other, Alex was uncertain of everything.

Chapter Two
Sibling Spotlight

When Alex walked back to the circular booth inside Clontz's café early Sunday morning, his iPhone pinged. He slipped the phone from the pocket of his khaki pants and then flopped down next to his younger brother Vincent. Sundays were Alex's favorite day of the week, even if yesterday's game hadn't played out exactly how he'd hoped.

"So, S.J.," Mrs. Tomassini stabbed the fork into her Asian sesame salad. "Have you thought about what college you would like to attend?"

Does mom have to bring this up now?

He leaned forward and held the phone with both hands. Rolling his eyes and scrolling through the numerous notifications, Alex wished it were his turn to tour schools, and the spotlight was on him.

Mrs. Tomassini was about three inches taller than Alex, with an athletic build and fair skin. She had long blonde hair, which she kept in a bun, and friendly blue eyes.

"Chapel Hill." S.J. gulped a fruit smoothie. "They have excellent major choices and an exceptional soccer program."

North Carolina was thousands of miles away.

He put his phone face down on the table, then crossed his arms. Alex understood why S.J. wanted to get out of Greenbriar. He couldn't shake the feeling he was the reason why S.J. was searching for an out-of-state school, much less a southern one.

S.J. was about six inches taller than Alex, with a sturdy build and olive skin like their dads. He had beady acorn brown eyes and short charcoal black hair that he kept brushing up.

"Is that the only one?" Mrs. Tomassini sipped her glass of iced water. "There are so many great schools like UConn Greenbriar and UCLA."

"Yes, mom," S.J. admitted. "As great as UConn Greenbriar is, it won't get me to the Pros."

"Which is what you have always wanted," Salvatore Tomassini bit his grilled chicken sandwich. "Otherwise, why would we have trained so hard for the last thirteen years."

Salvatore was tall and well-built with broad shoulders. He had short, curly charcoal black hair that he kept slicked back.

"Hey, dad." Alex stirred his bowl of Greek yogurt with strawberries and blueberries. "How'd that fundraiser go?"

"Much better than your game," Mr. Tomassini swallowed a few baked potato chips. "I heard you boys barely squeaked by."

"Yeah," Alex's face twisted in disappointment. "Allerton took us into overtime, but we managed to pull it off."

"Too close for comfort, though." S.J. nodded. "The way it looked from the stands, you guys struggled to make it up and down the field."

Alex shook his head. He recognized that the transition from summer baseball into soccer right away might be difficult. As he contemplated how not having time to condition much for fall sports hurt him and his pals, Alex was left with a sense of dread.

It's a matter of time before injuries pile up.

Hearing chatter nearby prompted Alex to turn his head and spot a trim girl with tanned skin and shoulder-length light, almost-blonde hair trotting toward their booth. He'd seen her before but couldn't place where. While noting the girl donned a "UConn Greenbriar shirt" tucked into a pair of light wash jeans, Alex wasn't sure which of his parents she came to see.

"Hey Hannah," Mrs. Tomassini poured more sesame sauce on her salad. "How are you?"

"I'm great," Hannah's smile lit up the room. "My classes are ok, but yours is my favorite; it's fun and relatable."

"You're too kind," Mrs. Tomassini wiped her face. "I do my best to make all lessons engaging and applicable for all students."

"The way I wish all courses were." Hannah pulled her phone from her jean pocket. "Anyhow, I'm taking a challenging political science elective and wondered if Senator Tomassini could take a look at the syllabus."

Someone always drags dad away.

Alex slipped his hands behind his head and let out a soft sigh. He hated how his dad consistently made time for everyone else except him. While he was bothered by his dad rarely attending games anymore, Alex could only hope that would change someday.

"Sure, thing Hannah," Mr. Tomassini held a hand before excusing himself. "I'll do whatever I can to help explain the course."

As he watched the two head off to a table close by, Alex shot his dad an icy glare that didn't go unnoticed.

"Dad would walk away," Alex turned and shook his head, "he doesn't care about my games."

"Yes, he does, honey," Mrs. Tomassini rubbed her son's back. "He can't help himself when someone wants to talk politics."

"Yeah, buddy," S.J. rested a hand on his younger brother's shoulder. "Don't beat yourself up over it."

"Maybe if we played better," Alex stared at his half-empty bowl with mixed fruit and yogurt remnants, "he'd show up once in a while."

Alex believed that too. He knew when professional sports teams went on droughts of losing seasons, their fans consistently abandoned them— well, most anyway. As he gave thought to what his dad might say about tweaking his hammy during their loss, Alex figured he'd omit that information.

Dad might give me one of those lectures about the importance of warming up.

"Trust me, sweetheart," Mrs. Tomassini guzzled down the rest of her iced water. "Your success or lack thereof on the field has no bearing on whether your father shows up or not."

"Right," S.J. nodded in agreement. "It's an election year, and he's constantly on the move with events to go to."

"Yeah, sure," Alex folded his arms and exhaled. "That must be it then."

"Don't worry, Alex," Vincent sat Indian-style now. "I'll always be there cheering you on."

Vincent was the family's baby and looked like their mom from the neck up with buzzed blonde hair. He was about a foot shorter than Alex, fair-skinned but was like a roadrunner from the looney tunes when it came to running. Playing soccer for Greenbriar United Soccer

Association and understanding more about soccer than its history, rules, and formations gave Vincent an advantage most kids his age didn't have. He never missed an opportunity to watch and learn how to improve his soccer prowess

Alex grabbed hold of his younger brother and hugged him. He couldn't have appreciated how supportive Vincent was. Although he realized he hadn't had much time to hang out, Alex knew he had to do better by him.

Twenty minutes later, Mr. Tomassini settled back at his seat in their booth.

"Sorry, Alex," Mr. Tomassini leaned forward with his hands folded. "We were discussing your game against Allerton."

"Yeah, Dad," Alex swallowed a lump in his throat. "I thought we'd win by more."

"As you should've," Mr. Tomassini tipped his head in contempt, "Especially with how weak you claimed the Falcons were."

"That was last year," Alex's face blushed as he shrugged his shoulders. "They must've improved."

Alex lied. He recognized that their opponents hadn't gotten better, but his team stumbled. Even while trying to honor his father according to God's commandments, Alex struggled to cope with the pressures of winning him over and not settling for second best in the family.

"Unlikely," S.J. pulled an arm across his chest. "You guys proved you were the better team, even by a slim margin. You guys will improve as the season goes on."

"Hear that, Alex?" Mr. Tomassini clapped and then pointed to his oldest son. "That's why S.J.'s the best in the family right there. He understands the game."

"Well," S.J. acted modestly, "and I've been where Alex is. It's not easy when you're on a talented team and are underperforming."

"Yup," Alex leaned back, "and it blows."

"Hang in, their pal," Mrs. Tomassini offered an encouraging smile. "This too shall pass."

Even if his family didn't come across as understanding and compassionate all the time, Alex knew they meant well. He'd always had a close relationship with his older brother and turned to him often. As he turned over the temporary problems with soccer in his mind, Alex knew things might get much worse before they got better.

#

Children shouted and laughed at the Reynolds Recreational Park as mothers chatted away on phones while simultaneously alerting their eyes to their toddlers. Groups of teenagers ranging in colors and sizes occupied basketball courts as they celebrated the weekend. Individuals and couples jogged around the concrete trail surrounding the perimeter of various empty fields offered by the complex. The temperatures were in the upper sixties with calm skies that brought ideal conditions for exercise.

Alex stepped onto this trail, soaked up all the scenery around with a smile, but stared straight ahead. Leaning forward and touching the tips of his white-and-blue running sneakers, he launched into a light jog. Hoping this interval training workout with S.J. would go better than the all-out chaos at lunch this afternoon,

At least he stood up for me earlier.

"Why do you want to go to Chapel Hill next year?" Alex swung his arms at his sides while relaxing his hands and shoulders. "You realize me and Vincent will be on our own with dad."

"Oh, Alex." S.J. turned to Alex and grinned. "Is my little brother going to miss me?"

Alex shook his head and sighed. He paused to collect himself and avoid saying something hurtful to his older brother. It would not matter, though, because S.J. had a way of brushing everything off. It gave Alex comfort that he could be himself with S.J., and no matter what he told him, he wouldn't get judged.

"No!" Alex lightly punched his older brother on the shoulder. "But it would be nice to have you around if I need advice and stuff."

"It's like this, Alex," S.J. evaluated his younger brother's running form, "I must get out of Greenbriar and out from under dad's vise grip if I expect to make a name for myself."

Since he turned four, S.J. had always been the big brother Alex resented yet wanted to live up to. He secretly admired him when they would work on drills in their backyard from the minute breakfast was over until the sun went down. Alex watched in awe as his older brother cut around the cones their dad set up. He shouted out, "Oooh snap," when S.J. fired shots into mini-goals.

"Even if it means abandoning us?" Alex scoffed. "It's hard enough to live up to the high standards, and it'll be nearly impossible to make dad proud."

"First of all, bro." S.J. pulled Alex toward him before inching off the trail. "I'd never abandon you guys, and I'm always a phone call away. Second, you should worry about being the best version of yourself, not mimicking everything I do on the field."

The brothers ran at a high-intensity pace for the next five minutes, where it was too difficult to hold a conversation. Once the first set concluded, the two continued jogging for a similar time before walking back to S.J.'s truck.

"Hey, S.J." Alex's hands were interlocked around his head as he caught his breath. "Can I ask you something?"

"What's that, squirt?" S.J. turned and cracked his knuckles.

"My buddy Connor's acted weird lately." Alex set his hands on his hips. "In our game the other day, he seemed out of it completely and snapped at me when I checked on him."

"That's odd." S.J. pushed a button on his car keys, and his truck's headlights began flashing. "Connor's still playing baseball as you all did over the summer, right? I bet he's just tired."

Alex knew his buddy's attitude and irritability were a much bigger deal than just fatigue. He'd reviewed their post-game hangout yesterday over and over in his head. While he wanted to dismiss everything that happened as Connor having a lousy day, Alex knew that couldn't have been further from the truth.

"That's the thing, though," Alex leaned forward and touched the tips of his sneakers before coming back up. "He's never gone off like that before. It's strange."

"Gone off?" S.J. made a face. "I don't understand."

"We're at the café after our game, right," Alex opened the passenger door and climbed inside, "and we started talking about class schedules for next week. When Phil and I mentioned loving Bible class, Connor said that studying the Bible was a waste of time."

"Which is isn't," S.J. climbed into the driver's seat. "There's so many nuggets of wisdom in the Bible and verses you can turn to in high and low times."

Alex completely agreed. He knew if there was anyone who'd understand how important religion classes were, it was his older brother. Although they sometimes interpreted verses differently because of their experiences, Alex found S.J.'s love for the lord admirable.

"Right, yeah," Alex tried not to get ahead of himself. "So, we found out that Connor's family stopped going to church and everything."

"Not good," S.J. jabbed his little brother on the shoulder. "If families stop attending church or fall away, it's because usually something bad happened or there was a crisis."

"I hope not," Alex hung his head. "Then we started talking about soccer, and he says he hasn't felt right since the season started."

"In what way?" S.J.'s eyes widened. "It's not unusual for kids your age to start burning out from sports they've participated in forever."

It was hard for Alex to imagine Connor burning out from sports. He knew that his teammate preferred baseball over soccer but never heard anything about not wanting to play anymore. As he considered if his buddy chose to focus on one sport exclusively now instead of two, Alex asked himself what that meant for their friendship.

"He doesn't enjoy playing anymore," Alex sighed, "and everything feels like a chore for him."

"I see," S.J.'s gaze bounced between the park entrance and his younger brother. "Has he told anyone?"

"Just our buddy Egan," Alex pushed a button and opened a window, letting the chilly breeze cool him down. "And Nick and I started telling him how we needed to be there for each other, and then he flipped out over us using scripture to cheer him up."

"Let me guess," S.J. responded like someone who'd experienced this situation a thousand times before, "you ask what's going on, and he storms out?"

Alex realized there was nothing he could tell S.J. that he hadn't heard before. He wasn't the type of kid who let much get to him; at least, that's what he showed others. As he thought about the situation more and realized he'd let his emotions get the best of him, Alex contemplated how much easier or more challenging things might get.

"Yup," Alex's face brightened. "How did you know?"

"It's happened to me hundreds of times, buddy," S.J. draped an arm around the passenger headrest. "A simple misunderstanding blows up into this huge disaster, and you end up not talking for days."

"See, this is why I need you around," Alex crackled. "What should I do?"

"Give Connor space," S.J. said immediately. "I know it sounds simple, but it's crucial right now. If you push him too hard, it might cause you guys to drift apart even further. He'll reach out when you least expect it."

For Alex, S.J. didn't need to say anything else. It was evident that his older brother understood what was going on. Even though the trials of middle school were more challenging than anything he'd ever faced on the field or court, Alex took comfort in knowing S.J. would be by his side through it all.

Chapter Three
Eighth Grade Expectations

Alex strutted across the campus of Beaumont Christian School on Tuesday morning. Although promptly assaulted by the humidity wrapping him up like a blanket, he felt a light breeze coming from tall trees nearby.

Approaching Humphrey Hall, the building devoted to middle schoolers, Alex exchanged high-fives and fist bumps with peers who complimented him on last week's win. Hearing mixtures of laughter and chattering fill the crowded hallways neared a set of lockers, Alex wondered what his first day of eighth grade had in store. He snatched supplies needed for the first four classes before securing the combination lock.

Why did I stay up so late watching Family Guy reruns? I barely had enough time to get ready before Dad dropped me off.

Alex slipped into first-period Bible Class after fifteen minutes of homeroom just before the warning bell. He took a seat in the front row, then gazed at the blackboard and saw "Old Testament" written. As he opened a binder and pulled out some notebook paper, Alex turned left to find a slightly taller and thicker boy with straight and shaggy dirty blond hair organizing materials. Sneaking a peek at the white paper beside his classmate that read "Landon Bettencourt, Fall 2011 semester schedule" made him smile.

"Hey, buddy," Alex rested his hands on the desk. "We missed you Saturday."

"Yeah, thanks," Landon grinned, revealing a mouthful of braces. "I was stuck in bed with an awful sinus infection."

"That stinks," Alex coughed into his elbow. "How are you feeling now?"

"Much better," Landon crossed a leg over the other and leaned back. "My grandfather told me we lost."

A barrel-chested older man with salt-and-pepper dark brown hair wearing a light-colored sweater and khakis, Alex recognized as Bishop Bettencourt, stepped inside.

"Good morning, class." Bishop Bettencourt wrote on the blackboard. "Welcome to eighth grade Old Testament class. As all of you should know, I'm Bishop Bettencourt, and I will be your teacher this semester. Although I've been here long enough that I had the pleasure of teaching your parents and siblings, my grandson Landon is new to the Beaumont Christian community this year. So please, make him feel welcome and help him find his classes if needed. Thanks!"

As Bishop Bettencourt continued speaking, Alex leaned back and listened. He believed in God the way some of his classmates didn't. While he sang hymns during services and followed along with Bible readings, Alex looked for the deeper meaning behind the texts.

I understand the Bible in the same way I do soccer.

"The Old Testament focuses on how our world came to exist, the Israelite's Exodus and the Ten Commandments," Bishop Bettencourt spoke with conviction. "While we traditionally start with Genesis, I thought it'd be better if we started looking at Proverbs 3:5-6. Who would like to start us off?"

"I will," Egan called out from the middle row.

"Thank you, Mister?" Bishop Bettencourt went down his attendance list.

"McCaskill," Egan confirmed. "Egan McCaskill! Trust in the Lord with all your heart, and do not lean on your own understanding. In all your ways, acknowledge him, and he will make straight your paths."

Even though it wasn't his favorite verse, Alex knew there was a reason Bettencourt picked it. He saw the relevance in his relationships with close friends and soccer season itself. As he took apart the text piece by piece, it forced Alex to contemplate if he'd only leaned on his understanding rather than trusting the lord.

"Great reading Egan," Bishop Bettencourt settled onto his desk with his long legs hanging. "Let's go around the room and see what this verse means to some of you."

Egan raised his hand first. "If we trust God and acknowledge his presence, he'll guide us."

"Don't try to understand everything yourself," Alex extended his arm and then answered. "But trust that God will show us the way."

"You boys are on the right track," Bishop Bettencourt encouraged the class. "The first thing this verse tells us is 'trust in the Lord with all your heart, and do not lean on your understanding.' That trust part is so difficult for everyone, including me."

The best part about Alex's Bible class was how verses were broken down, and everyone understood. He benefitted from Bettencourt's ability to draw students in and relate the material to daily happenings. While puzzling over what classes were next, Alex knew Bettencourt's Bible class was the best.

Soon after Bible class, Alex trotted over to Sullivan Science and Technology Center for his following two courses. He had his newest teammate on his mind and mulled over how they hadn't gotten to know each other. Although they weren't friends, Alex knew the right thing to do was lend a hand in whatever way he could.

As he approached Mrs. Conway's second-period Science, Alex looked over his shoulder and caught sight of Landon following close behind.

"You've got Conway too?" Alex extended out a closed fist. "That's awesome."

"Yup," Landon bumped his teammate's fist. "What are the odds, right?"

"Heck, if I know," Alex joked. "I hate math."

"Ditto," Landon matched strides with Alex. "It's the worst."

Even while taking notes from start to finish, Alex ruminated over how great a start to the day it'd been. It was almost a welcome distraction given how this class compared to an honor level one nobody expected. At speed, they'd reviewed their syllabus, course expectations, and policies; Alex wondered if Conway held a Ph.D. in addition to the required bachelor's.

Just as he'd put science in the rearview mirror, Alex focused his attention on mathematical concepts. He looked forward to Coach Schallhorn's Algebra 1 about as much as stretching before team workouts.

Waste of time, but we've got to do it.

After what seemed like an eternity of viewing an algebraic movie trailer, Alex breathed a sigh of relief, entering fourth-period Film Appreciation back at Humphrey Hall. Eager to be lost in discussions about some terrific movies, Alex smiled when their teacher Mr. McEnaney ran through the syllabus. Although papers were due every Friday on assigned movies, Alex looked forward to breaking from the usual subjects.

A fine arts class where we watch films, what could be better?

Once class concluded, Alex exited the classroom and tucked supplies under his arm. He trotted down the crowded hallways, and his stomach growled. While turning a corner and moving toward his locker, Alex saw Connor leaning against a wall.

"Hey Alex," Connor said. "We need to talk."

##

Inside the spacious lunchroom at Ertter Events, students stood in line to punch their desired lunch choices on kiosks. Mixtures of laughter and chattering rang out. Various smells permeated the busy kitchen. Staff members delivered kiosk-ordered meals to select students.

"Are you serious, Al?" Nick woofed down a tuna sandwich. "Con doesn't want to sit with us anymore?"

"That's what he told me." Alex doused a chicken tender in some ranch. "Connor said he didn't want to hang out with people who bring him down. He'd rather sit with Egan."

"Nah," Nick shook his head. "That sounds like an excuse."

"Yeah," Phil chewed on an apple slice covered in peanut butter. "Con man's only saying that because of what happened at the café. He's too sensitive."

All three sat around a high-top table on bar-style stools in the right corner of the lunchroom.

Alex agreed. With their dads being such close friends, he understood first-hand how demanding Connor's dad was. It was hard sometimes for Alex to see his friend acting so miserable. If Connor was honest about his feelings toward soccer, quitting the team made sense to Alex. But if his pal was still mad from last week, that was worse. Either way, Alex thought, it wasn't good for their friendship or the Rams.

"Right, yeah." Alex wasn't the type to subscribe to gossip. He'd familiarized himself with Proverbs 16:28, which read, "a perverse person stirs up conflict, and a gossip separates close friends." While realizing how hurtful talking about Connor was, Alex decided to change the subject. "What is everyone's favorite and least favorite classes?"

"Social Studies," Nick spoke first. "Gentry relates the past and the present to explain the material."

"Bettencourt's Bible class for me," Alex's face brightened. "He not only reads the verses but asks what they mean to us."

"That's dope," Phil swigged a water bottle. "I love McEnaney's film class."

Alex admitted that Film Appreciation was his second favorite. He enjoyed getting lost in almost any movie, especially mystery and horror. As he imagined himself in Shutter Island, a film he'd seen with Phil and his dad last year, Alex grinned at the idea of him and his best friend investigating an escaped patient at Ashe Cliffe Hospital.

At that instant, Alex spotted Kellen strutting over with a large smirk. He remembered his teammate had carried himself that way ever since their Greenbriar United days. Although Kellen was an incredible soccer player whose performance and voice spoke loudest on the field, Alex admitted he was one of those kids you tolerated.

"Yo broskis." Kellen glanced at the three teammates and nodded. "Where's Con-air?"

"Probably with Egan." Nick shrugged his shoulders. "Con told us he was losing interest in soccer, though."

"Is that so?" Kellen tipped his chin up in a snobby manner. "We've got training today, and he'd better be there."

"Right." Nick twisted around to look behind. "What does your dad have planned anyway?"

"Core and Cardio," Kellen propped his hands on his hips. "We'll split into two groups like always, one doing speed exercises while another is doing crunches and stuff."

"Oh joy," Phil forced a smile. "I can hardly wait."

Alex shared his best friend's dread about training. He was never a fan of how intense training sessions were at times. While reminiscing about how hard Coach Schallhorn ran, he and his pals as sixth graders left Alex unsure how they made it through.

Those days were the worst.

"Something funny, Larson?" Kellen sported a smug expression.

"Watching you condition," Phil giggled, "reminds me of a duck waddling."

"Darn," Nick laughed alongside his friend. "He's got, you big guy."

"Pssh," Kellen folded his arms across his chest. "Whatever you say, short stuff."

Alex loved what he saw. He knew if there was one thing he and his buddies could agree on, their shared opinion of the coach's son. Even though he took soccer and everything that came with it seriously, Alex understood there was never a lousy time for humor.

When their teammate trotted away, Phil uttered, "I can't stand that kid!"

Chapter Four
Warnings of Weariness

As Alex dashed over to Vitello Athletic Center beside Phil later that same afternoon; he mulled over the conversation with Connor and his pal's analysis and was baffled. It'd swirled around his mind during Phys ed, Spanish, Social Studies, and Language Arts. Even while approaching the double-door entrance and setting foot in, Alex's heartbeat doubled in speed over where their teammate was.

"What'd you think of our last few classes?" Alex said, hurrying up a flight of stairs. "Social Studies class was my favorite."

"I love Language Arts," Phil matched his teammate's strides, then turned, "but I can't stand Farnsworth."

"Ditto," Alex made a sour face. "She's old school."

"Yup," Phil smiled, his pearly white teeth gleamed, "otherwise why would she have assigned a five-page paper on the first day?"

Alex admitted that discussing classes and teachers was a welcome distraction. He'd been so worried about their teammate recently that it tormented him. While picturing how little effort Connor might give during their session and Coach Schallhorn's reaction to it, it left Alex's chest tightening.

"Someone who hates kids," Alex rolled his neck around, "and the idea of free time or extracurriculars."

"Right," Phil nodded in agreement. "It'll be a long semester."

"You can say that again," Alex groaned. "At least we've got soccer to look forward to."

"Yup," Phil rolled his shoulders. "Thank god for that."

While crossing through the bright gymnasium and heading for the locker room closet to Beaumont Christian's fitness center, Alex breathed a sigh of relief. He couldn't wait to get started training. Even though sitting through eight hours of teachers lecturing about their subjects wasn't all that bad, it allowed Alex time to get out of his head.

As he opened the door and moved into the large area behind his best friend, Alex heard voices nearby. He turned and gazed at Connor and Egan at the opposite end. While swapping his school uniform out for workout gear, Alex ran a hand underneath his sore hamstring and cringed.

"I swear, dude," Connor pulled an arm across his chest, "if my dad chews me out one more time, I'm running away."

"Don't!" Egan's voice cracked. "I already told you that you can stay with us anytime you need to escape."

"I know," Connor's shoulders dropped. "But my dad won't allow any sleepovers when I'm with him

"Dang, bud," Egan ran his fingers through his messy dark brown hair. "What a jerk!"

Alex couldn't believe it. He'd never expected his teammate's problems were family-related. As he exchanged looks with Phil, who'd planted himself beside him and shook his head, Alex's eyes almost came out of their sockets.

What the heck?

Hearing footsteps approaching and then turning, Alex saw Connor and Egan trotting past them but paused.

"Don't say anything," Connor put on a poker face. "If it gets around that my parents are having trouble, everything will worsen."

"Trust me," Alex swallowed a lump in his throat. "I won't tell anyone."

"Ditto, bro," Phil offered a reassuring smile. "We've got your back."

"We'll see you guys there," Egan patted Connor's back. "We're going to start warming up."

Alex's heart sank while studying his comrades filing out of the locker room. He'd only overheard part of their teammate's conversation, but enough to warrant concern. As he pondered if there was anything he could do to help, Alex knew his choices were limited.

#

Beaumont Christian's fitness center was bright and buzzing minutes later. Elliptical machines, treadmills, and cycling bikes were stationed to the left, while weight machines and free weights lay across long racks located on the right. Near padded walls lay long rubber mats for stretching, resistance band exercises, foam rollers, and core exercises in the back. Several agility ladders, cones, a giant box, and dots were arranged between aerobic and weight machines stationed throughout the area. Drake's Headlines resonated from a fancy stereo system as Coach Schallhorn strode around, studying the boys' technique and offering constructive criticism.

As Alex approached a five-foot-high box, his muscles twitched with excitement. He leaped onto the box and kept his knees over his toes. While landing safely on the top and jumping back down then up again without ceasing until he finished up, Alex felt his legs ache.

He remembered the first time doing agility drills. When his dad introduced him and S.J. about seven years ago, nothing could've been more exciting than seeing an obstacle course of fitness equipment spread throughout the Tomassini backyard. As he learned the importance of staying healthy and focused as a youth athlete, it gave Alex the mental strength needed during days like these.

"Keep going," he mumbled to himself while springing onto the box and landing with both feet on the floor. "Don't give up."

These are squash exercises, Alex thought. Please *give me something more challenging.*

"Awesome job," Phil slapped his best friend a high-five. "You crushed those box jumps."

"Yeah," Alex leaned up and grabbed a sizeable blue thermos set off to the side, then chugged it. "They're cakewalk."

"Sure are," Phil rested a hand on Alex's shoulder and pulled a leg toward his behind. "But our game Thursday won't be. That's why we can't overtrain."

"Definitely," Alex nodded. "We can't afford any injuries."

Alex still hadn't told anyone about his sore leg. It wasn't something he'd considered a huge deal with their record. Even as he weighed letting Vance know, Alex realized he'd hear an earful about any vulnerabilities from his dad.

While strolling toward a hallway separating the fitness center and gymnasium beside Phil, Alex turned and gave his teammates a once-over. He took note of how much taller and bigger Nick and Xavier were. Although he knew everyone grew and developed at their own pace, Alex wondered when it'd be his turn.

"Time for core exercises next," Phil motioned to the Ram starters trotting over to the rubber mat. "I hate them so much."

"Yeah," Alex sipped his thermos. "They're exhausting."

"At least the girls will start noticing us," Phil smiled, "even if it's only at the pool."

Alex knew what his pal meant. Since Beaumont Christian was an all-boys school for as long as he'd remembered, the only time they saw girls were off-campus, at visiting team's fields or the country club where their families were members. Even though he'd started noticing how pretty girls their age were, Alex hadn't found the courage to ask any out.

"They already have," Alex nudged Phil on the shoulder. "Erin told me that Maddie was totally into you."

"Forreal?" Phil's eyes widened. "I thought she only talked to me since we both liked One Tree Hill."

"Nope," Alex held out a closed fist. "She likes you."

"Sweet," Phil bumped his teammate's fist. "Maybe I do have a shot."

As far back as Alex remembered, his best friend never missed an opportunity to chat up with girls. It didn't matter if it was during a lunch break at a sub shop during a Greenbriar United Soccer tournament. If his buddy spotted a girl, he'd talk. While his older brother gave him tips on talking to the opposite sex, Alex always seemed tongue-tied and messed up, especially if a girl was stunning.

Alex settled onto the mats in the back next to Phil, following a brief water break. He noticed their group moved onto another movement called windshield wipers. As he lifted his legs and bent his knees, Alex strained every muscle to rotate his hips to one side before returning to the starting point.

"Looking good, boys," Coach Schallhorn clapped while studying the Ram players. "Keep that back flat, and don't forget to breathe out when rotating your hips."

"These exercises suck, dude," Phil whispered. "My lower back's tensing up so bad."

"Same," Alex twisted his face in discomfort. "I'm looking forward to whatever conditioning Schallhorn has planned."

"Yup," Phil's legs dropped with a smack. "Anything's better than this."

While progressing through multiple sets of three more movements, Alex glanced at Connor, giving it his all. He noticed his friend's pained expressions with every move. As he thought about how stressed out, Connor must be at home, coming to school had to take a toll on him. Alex knew it couldn't be easy.

In that same instant, he heard howls and shouts nearby. A grin emerged as he'd lifted his head and saw another teammate, Landon, hopping on one foot from one dot to another almost effortlessly without losing balance. Even though he and Connor were still buddies, Alex admitted that their reserve teammate might give them the best chance to win.

I'd never tell Connor that. It'd tear him apart.

A whistle shrilled, drowning out the hip-hop music thumping nearby.

"Alright, boys," Coach Schallhorn hollered from some weight machines. "Take a breather, and we'll meet in the gym for our final drill."

Even as the Ram players got to their feet and headed in the gymnasium's direction, Alex remained on his right side. He hadn't recovered from the lying side hip exercises yet. Holding an arm up and waving a hand around forced Alex to consider how winded he was.

"Let's go, buddy," Phil grabbed hold of his teammate's hand. "One more drill until we stretch."

"Good," Alex let Phil help him back up. "I'm so stiff right now."

"Me too," Phil groaned. "I hope all of our training pays off."

"It'd better," Alex's gaze struck the royal blue Ram logo above the entranceway, "or the Eagles will run circles around us."

Alex knew their team's biggest problem thus far was lack of endurance. The matchup in two days wasn't important from a record standpoint since they were undefeated. It was significant because they'd struggled to close out their last game during regulation. Although team morale wasn't awful, Alex sensed it'd worsen if teammates' tensions continued mounting.

Every Rams player had split into two groups in the gymnasium in just fifteen minutes. Additional cones on both sides joined eight orange cones set up in a straight line three feet apart. Coach Schallhorn instructed Kellen to demonstrate the drill.

Just as Kellen raced from one cone to another, Coach Schallhorn evaluated his son's technique, "quicker strides, don't turn toward that cone!"

After that, boys from either group stepped up for their turns. The first round found Phil facing off with Nick.

"Go!" Coach Schallhorn hollered from a set of bleachers.

Alex leaned against the wall and stared. Watching his friends compete was like viewing WWE or UFC for him, no matter who won. Despite Phil being shorter and skinner than Nick, Alex admired how fluid his best friend glided across the field or court.

Alex's heart pounded, focusing on Connor moving forward in line. He'd consistently noticed his close friends' strides resembled Frankenstein: all stiffened up. Since he hadn't partnered up with Connor during workouts or training sessions recently, Alex didn't know if his teammate hid an injury.

At that moment, Alex spotted his best friend hobbling over with a pained expression. He extended a hand and then pulled him toward the wall. While sizing up his teammate, Alex sensed Phil might've turned the wrong way.

Even as Phil dropped to a knee and bent forward from hip to knee, Alex heard his teammate sigh. He pushed him ahead, hoping it helped. While studying Phil's uneasy movements, Alex prayed his best bud wasn't hurt.

"Thanks," Phil exhaled, holding onto his teammate's arm as he got to his feet. "My quad tightened up when I lunged on that last cone."

"I could tell something wasn't right," Alex turned and frowned. "You, okay?"

"I will be," Phil rested a hand on Alex's shoulder and pulled a leg toward his behind. "Thanks."

"Yup," Alex patted Phil on the back. "You know I've got your back."

Alex recalled the pact he and Phil made in their early days at Beaumont Christian. They'd promised to remain friends and be there for each other no matter what, which only strengthened their bond. Although they weren't family or anything, Alex thought of Phil not only as his best friend but as a brother. It wasn't only because they two played sports together or spent a lot of time outside of athletics hanging out either.

Within seconds, Phil nudged Alex on the shoulder and then said, "Check out Connor and Landon, squaring off."

Alex turned to see the two boys moving around the cones. He knew these two teammates were different in many ways. As he noted how Landon's lightning-fast speed while changing directions and Connor's lack of energy, it was clear to Alex that his pal's troubles impacted him more than he knew.

Alex nodded in awe, almost in concert, as Landon spun around the final cone and grazed its top. Connor, on the other hand, found himself finishing a distant second.

"Dadgummit," Connor shouted, striking the padded wall. "What the f— is wrong with me?"

"Mr. Snodgrass," Coach Schallhorn's voice bounced off the white brick walls. "See me after training."

"But coach," Connor's face blushed. "I've got base—"

"It wasn't a request," Coach Schallhorn flashed his player a dirty look.

Chapter Five
Gameday Groans

As Alex squeezed between Connor and Phil on the cold concrete floor in the visitor's locker room of Dunleavy Charter School's soccer field, his heart pounded. He caught a whiff of sweat, antiseptic, and icy/hot patches that left his nose itching. As he surveyed the large area with teammates scattered around with glazed away looks on their faces and strained to breathe, it left Alex wondering how they'd survive the second half.

It was late afternoon on Thursday when Beaumont Christian squared off with Dunleavy Charter School in a game that most agreed should've been canceled. There had been a thunderstorm in the wee hours of the morning and stretched until only four hours ago that submerged all athletic fields. Both teams played through and managed some goals despite these hazardous conditions. While there was still one-half remaining after intermission, neither squad intended to let up.

"Come on, boys," Coach Schallhorn said, standing beside a whiteboard in front of the area. "You've got to get it together on the field. Quicken the pace and make smarter passes. We'll catch them off guard. Keep sprinting hard across the field. Watch out for those slide tackles. I know some of you were banged up. On defense, you've got to support Egan better. He's running himself ragged, trying to stop all the shots that came his way."

Alex had taken a beating. His formerly crisp white jersey and shorts were caked with mixtures of mud and grass. As he'd faked and slashed across the field, Alex had slipped countless times when his legs gave way or cleats got bogged down.

In the front row, with his legs stretched out ahead of him, Alex titled forward and touched the tips of his mud-coated cleats. He felt his legs throbbing the further he went. While trying to alleviate the discomfort in his legs and limber up, Alex heard grunting close by.

"Gosh darn," Connor brought the soles of his cleats together, then bent onward. "I can't get loose today."

"Need some help?" Alex turned to his teammate.

"No," Connor scowled. "Not from you."

"Fine," Alex shook his head in confusion. "I don't want to see you injured."

Alex wasn't sure what was up. He'd noted his teammates' frustration worsened. While weighing if Connor hurt himself during training or at some point today, Alex felt more puzzled at his buddy rejecting any help.

As he'd readjusted and then tipped ahead, Alex smacked the floor. He couldn't seem to ease the stiffness in his legs either. While lying down now and staring at the bright ceiling, Alex considered that he was sorer than he even knew.

"Hey, dude," Phil sat beside him with his hands hanging over his knees. "Did you want some help stretching before we hit the field?"

"Sure, yeah," Alex massaged his temples. "I can barely move, much less lift my legs."

"Yup," Phil raised his best bud's leg and extended it. "That happens when you lay on the floor during halftime."

"I tried loosening up before," Alex flinched, "but nothing worked."

While asking himself if he should tell Vance, Alex heard a shrill whistle and turned his head. He saw Coach Schallhorn standing in the center of the room, holding a clipboard. Even as he grasped Phil's hand and assisted up, Alex imagined the second half being more challenging and brutal.

"Alright, boys," Coach Schallhorn clapped. "Finish up with whatever you're doing and head back onto the field. It's game time!"

The Ram players immediately trotted toward the locker room door in groups, with Alex leading the pack. He matched strides with his best friend and stared ahead at the field illuminated by bright, vivid lights above. As he heard the Beaumont Christian fans erupt into cheers in the away stands and cleats clacking on concrete walkways, Alex remembered his two favorite soccer soundtracks.

"Let's go!" Alex screamed, sprinting onto Dunleavy Charter's soccer field with his teammates following closely.

# #

Alex hustled across the center mark of Dunleavy Charter's soccer field. He barely avoided a thick puddle of muddy water and then felt an opponent wallop into him. As he scouted out open teammates, Alex caught sight of Connor, on the right, who'd just spun past a defender and streaked along the touchlines.

"Over here," Alex Connor said, waving an arm around. "I'm open, bro!"

While sending a pass in his teammate's direction, Alex tumbled over and came down face first. He felt the air deflate from his lungs and strained for breath. Lifting his head to find Connor lunging ahead only to have the ball land and bounce out of play forced Alex to consider if his friend should even be playing.

Gosh, darn it!

The whistle blew as Alex pushed himself up.

"Throw in, green!" the referee motioned to Dunleavy Charter's touchline.

Alex studied Connor approaching with a limp, favoring his leg. It was the same issue his teammate tried loosening during intermission but didn't look any better off. As he shook his head and shrugged his shoulders, Alex wondered whether there was anything he could say that wouldn't escalate tensions further.

"Come on, man," Alex stretched out a closed fist. "How'd you miss that pass?

"My flipping groin," Connor bumped his teammate's fist. "I can't loosen it for anything."

"Why didn't you take my help or ask Vance?" Alex made a face. "You know how important it is to stick together."

"Yeah, well," Connor sighed. "I thought I could do it on my own."

Alex knew his buddy's attitude issues were starting to evolve. It wasn't enough that his teammate played poorly and acted negatively, but now he was hurt. As he weighed whether to scream at Connor to sub out before he was sorry, Proverbs 14:29 came to Alex's mind.

The whistle blew as an Eagle player hoisted the ball over his head and scanned the field.

"Alex, Connor," Coach Schallhorn hollered from the away touchlines, "quit yapping and look alive."

Alex turned his attention to an opponent in a dark green jersey tossing a pass toward the center circle. He heard his heart pound as if it were about to explode from his chest. Even as a shooting pain erupted from the back of his leg, Alex flashed forward toward the incoming sphere.

Let's go! Whatever it takes!

Leaping in front of an opponent and taking the ball off his knee in Eagle territory, Alex heard Ram fans break out in cheers. He dribbled ahead and saw his best friend faking right, then feint past a defender on the left. As he let a pass to Phil fly, Alex snuck a peek at the scoreboard, which showed 1-1 with less than ten minutes to play in regulation.

"Come on, Pal," Alex clapped his hands. "You've got this."

Simultaneously, Alex turned back to see Phil gathering the ball off his cleat and then slashing past a larger Eagle player. He surveyed with great interest as his buddy pulled the ball back and fired a shot.

That has to be a goal.

The ball sailed toward the goal and veered right. Dunleavy Charter's goalie raced over then captured it before colliding with the goal post.

Alex's heart sank. He observed the goalie roll out to an Eagle midfielder. As he saw his opponent approaching in haste, Alex galloped at an angle to catch him.

Within seconds, fans from both sides held their breaths when Alex and his Eagle counterpart crashed into each other outside Dunleavy Charter's penalty box, sending the ball bouncing away.

At that moment, Phil gathered the ball off his shin guard and fired a pass to Xavier, who lobbed a shot.

The ball floated a short distance to the goal and swerved left. Dunleavy Charter's goalie sprinted in its direction and dove in front, swatting the ball away.

Almost immediately, Phil dashed forward and met the ball just as it arrived inside the penalty box and popped a shot.

The ball drifted over to the goal and rippled against the net.

The whistle blew as Ram players celebrated their goal.

Alex had recovered slowly near the center circle and was back on a knee. He used both hands to push himself back up and saw his opponent still down, clutching his knee and shaking. As he staggered over to the Eagle midfielder whose cries sent goosebumps up his arms, Alex was compelled to wave over Dunleavy Charter's bench for an athletic trainer.

"Hang in there, dude," Alex patted his opponent on the leg. "It'll be ok."

While limping over to join his teammates, Alex thought through Proverbs 24:17 about not rejoicing when an enemy falls and not letting your heart rejoice when they stumble. He didn't view any opponents they faced as enemies but felt awful for Dunleavy Charter. Even as the back of his leg throbbed beyond belief, Alex realized there was always somebody worse off.

"You, ok?" Phil slapped his teammate a high-five and then studied him. "That was a nasty collision."

"I'll live," Alex gave a reassuring grin. "I'm glad we scored."

"Right, Al," Nick interlocked his hands around his head to catch his breath, "off a rebound no less."

"Tough loss for the Eagles," Phil lay a hand on Alex's shoulder, then pulled a leg toward his behind. "It looks like he got the worse of the tackle."

Alex winced. He wasn't sure why his buddy thought that since he and the Eagle player went down. Even though he walked away, Alex didn't consider himself lucky either, not in the least.

Coach Schallhorn blew his whistle and gestured for the team to gather around.

"Can you help me to the touchlines?" Alex nudged Phil on the shoulder. "I'm alright, but I could use a hand."

"Yeah, sure," Phil matched strides with his teammate, "no problem."

"Don't let coach see," Alex dangled an arm around Phil's shoulder. "I've got to stay on the field."

"No worries," Phil nodded. "I've got your back."

As he stood in a circle beside his teammates with hands propped on his hips, Alex mulled over if he'd finish the game. He knew Schallhorn wouldn't take out starters, especially with a close score. While looking over his buddies' exhausted faces, Alex couldn't help but wonder how they felt.

"Incredible tenacity, boys," Coach Schallhorn gave the Ram players a once over, "you kept pushing yourselves until you scored. Way to bounce back from the turnover earlier and turn it into a scoring opportunity. That was an amazing defensive effort and one heck of a tackle, Alex."

Even as Coach Schallhorn carried on with his observations, Alex noted how Connor wasn't called out. He realized that his teammates probably felt awful enough as it was, injury or not. While turning to his pal, whose head hung low and shoulders slumped, Alex dwelled on what ate at him.

When the whistle blew around nine minutes later and ended their game, a final score of 3-2 showed on the scoreboard in favor of Beaumont Christian. As both teams lined up to shake hands, Alex felt a hand rest on his shoulder, then turned to find Connor standing behind.

"Oh, hey," Alex smiled. "Sup bud?"

"Can you guys come over Saturday?" Connor swallowed a lump in his throat. "I've got something to tell you."

Chapter Six
Uneasiness Uncovered

Alex's hands gripped a PlayStation 3 controller, which directed the movement of private investigator Scott Shelby stepping through the front door entrance of a run-down motel. As he approached the front desk and asked the clerk where his client Lauren White's room was, Scott turned the corner and climbed the stairs. He walked down a smoke-blanketed hallway on the second floor.

"Yo Al." Nick handed Alex a large bag of vegetable chips. "Have you seen the promos for Criminal Minds?

"I may have." Alex tapped the controller's buttons. "It picks up right where last season left off, right?"

"Yep, with the blackouts in Los Angeles," Nick smiled. "Where the unsub takes out detective Garret."

"I remember." Alex ran a hand through his spiky gelled hair. "It'll be a great season."

"The best yet," Nick focused his attention on the game where Scott and Lauren talked about their mutual enemy, the Origami Killer. I'm stoked, man."

Nick and Alex were sitting on a small couch in the Snodgrass living room early Sunday afternoon with their legs propped up on recliners. They played video games on a fifty-five-inch flat screen mounted on a beige wall. Phil sat on the floor with his arms hanging over his knees while Connor stretched his legs out on a recliner nearby, observing the game's storyline.

Alex paused to watch Scott leave Lauren's room and stroll toward the stairs. Watching Scott get things done made Alex wish he were his older brother's age and heading to college next year. He wouldn't major in political science or pre-law like S.J., but maybe he could pursue media studies or English and forge his legacy.

Suddenly, the controller vibrated as Scott clutched his throat with both hands and dropped to a knee. Alex tapped the buttons as fast as he could manage and followed the flurry of on-screen prompts. Meanwhile, a skinny guy with a tank top and jeans stomped past Scott and banged on Lauren's door. Scott crawled to his feet and strode toward Lauren's room after hearing piercing screams. Scott grappled the attacker before throwing him across the room, and Alex pressed buttons furiously to keep the bad guy at bay until he kicked the wall before exiting the room. Alex set the controller down and wiped his brow as the game transitioned to a cut scene. He, Nick, and Phil had come over at the invitation of Connor, who'd said he needed some company, but it made them wonder if their friend was about to spill some beans.

"Gee whiz Connor," Phil said, readjusting his chino shorts that rode up his legs. "How are you allowed to play this game?"

Heavy Rain was rated Mature, and all the boys were on the wrong side of 17. Alex was expecting to hear about what scheme Connor had hatched, and he was getting ready to call bull on it. Instead, Connor sat straight and gazed distantly, suggesting something gigantic was coming.

"A year ago, I wouldn't have been," he explained. "But my parents started fighting, and things like what kind of games I played didn't matter. Once they got divorced a few months back, they'd give me anything I wanted. I guess they worried that I'd hate them or run away."

Everyone was silent while Connor's words hung heavily in the air. Alex thought briefly of his parents. His dad was very seldom home, but they'd never split.

"I'm sorry, Con," Nick looked at the gleaming hardwood floors. "What happened?"

"The fighting started a few years back, and it just kept getting worse," Connor's voice cracked. "That's why we stopped going to church. I've had a real hard time, and Egan's been there for me. His family practically took me in when everything started."

"You never said anything." Alex gave Connor the controller. "I had no idea things were that bad for you."

"Yeah, well," Connor told him, "It's not something you want to advertise. You can understand why I didn't want to be around anyone either, not the soccer team. They're so judgmental and yappy."

Back on the screen, FBI Agent Jayden Norman rolled his sedan to a stop as the rain continued slapping onto the windshield like a writer pounding the keys on a keyboard. Stepping out of the car and flashing identification, agent Jayden ducked under the yellow tape. He headed toward the small tent where the latest victim of the Origami Killer lay. The more Alex looked at Connor's facial expressions toward the game, the angrier he noticed his pal become, and the more Alex wanted to intervene.

What can I do to help?

"I just don't understand why everything keeps going wrong," Connor shook his head. "First, it's my parents, then soccer, and now I might lose my spot."

"Yeah, Con." Nick sat up straight. "That's a lot to deal with at once."

"Tell me about it," Connor interlocked his hands behind his head and stretched. "And to make matters worse, Schallhorn threatened to bench me if I don't start playing better and my attitude doesn't improve."

"Dang," Phil gazed at their friend and tightened his lips. "Maybe it's for the best; if we aren't the best versions of ourselves, we can't help anyone else. And lately, you're snapping at everybody."

"Shut up, Phil." Connor fired back. "You'd be worn out and stressed too if your parents shuffled you back and forth more times than a piece of luggage."

The game switched to a scene where another protagonist, Ethan Mars, was undergoing a psychotherapist session. As images flashed across the screen seemingly every second and drew Alex's attention back to his friend's living room, he wondered what was going through Connor's head.

Would he break down and admit he needed support from friends? Or would he keep his anger and frustrations bottled up? Connor is like a ticking time bomb in action movies, Alex thought. *He'll explode if nobody helps.*

Scanning the living room, Alex realized only he and Connor were sitting down as the other two took bathroom breaks and went to grab more snacks. It was the perfect time for Alex to chat privately with his teammate.

"Hey, buddy." Alex slapped Connor's knee. "Is there anything I can do to help?"

"Stop my dad from riding me," Connor clenched his fists and stared at the hardwood floor. "I swear, dude, I don't know what to do anymore. I can't stand it when he belittles everything I do. And it's all because I'm not living up to the 'Snodgrass' name."

Alex, of course, knew better than most what his teammate was referring to. Even though he only had one older brother who constantly trended upward in their dad's eyes, it was enormous pressure. Unable to imagine having to live up to the accolades of three older brothers, all of whom attended prominent universities and were excellent athletes, and a dad who was impossible to please sometimes forced Alex to consider whether he had it all that bad. However awful things seemed, he remembered his mom always saying someone else's situation was worse than yours.

The words routinely came across as dismissive to Alex until he started participating in more out-of-state sports tournaments, where he became exposed to people and places outside Greenbriar. During these times, Alex witnessed the acts of kindness and charity his parents preached as a rule. Rightfully as crucial as the number of service opportunities offered by Beaumont Christian School with the hope of showing students like him in less fortunate circumstances.

While shooting baskets in the driveway of his family's home early Sunday evening, Alex considered how to help his close friend. He'd realized how much his teammates' situation hampered him during school and soccer. As his mind drifted back to how down and frustrated Connor was when he and his buddies hung out earlier, Alex wished there was more he could do to cheer him up.

At that moment, the front door opened, and S.J. emerged. He trotted toward his younger brother and paused near the garage door before clapping his hands.

Taking a pass in with both hands and squaring up toward the high basketball hoop, S.J. fired a shot with a wrist flick.

The basketball glided toward the crisp white net and floated through.

"Nice!" Alex gathered the rebound and lofted a pass back to his older brother. "Did you come to shoot around with me?"

"Nah, brother." S.J. launched another similar shot. "Mom asked me to get you so you could wash up and set the table for dinner."

"Alright." Alex rebounded the ball and, in a second, tipped it off the glass. "Can I just take a few more shots, please?"

"Of course, Alex," S.J. motioned for him to run toward the basketball for a layup. "I know you only come out and shoot around when you need to clear your head. Is something on your mind?"

Although S.J. was somewhat aware of everything with his close friend, Alex hadn't told him everything. He loved his older brother and came to him for advice. In this instance, however, Alex wanted to try and figure everything out on his own, even as challenging as that might be. To avoid getting into a conversation that might follow the two into the kitchen, he decided to play it cool.

"Just school stuff and soccer." Alex faked left and cut right past an imaginary defender as S.J. sent him a bounce pass that he flicked off his fingertips. "No biggie, bro."

Except this was a big deal for Alex, a much bigger deal than he was willing to admit at this moment.

"Whatever you're dealing with, buddy," S.J. said supportively. "It'll all be ok."

Chapter Seven
Overridden by Obsession

By the time he stepped through Sullivan Science and Technology Center's entrance on Wednesday morning, Alex's mind was on his team's upcoming game against Greenbriar Day. As he trotted down a long hallway and rounded the corner, Alex wondered what game plan Coach Schallhorn was cooking up. He slipped into science class just before the warning bell rang. *Whatever coach has scheduled for us, it'll be a lot of running.*

He settled at his usual seat next to Nick. Going through the motions of notetaking and only half hearing Mrs. Conway's lecture on atoms and molecules, Alex related the relation between two or more atoms bonding together and the Rams soccer team. *Nick, Landon, and Phil were like protons, while Connor and Kellen were electrons, negatively charged particles.*

Aside from winning and being the best, it was hard for Alex to find motivation during soccer games. Scanning the bleachers throughout their last few contests, all of which they'd won, Alex only found his mom, S.J., and Vincent. Alex's heart sank, learning his dad had missed their latest game, where he'd scored the winning goal.

Why doesn't dad want to see me play? He asked himself. *Are my games not important?*

"Yo Al." Nick nudged his classmate's shoulder. "Did you hear what I said?"

Alex hadn't heard anything. Gazing at the periodic table of elements nearby, lost in thought, he couldn't help but visualize a soccer field and, beyond it, the scoreboard. A scoreboard he hoped existed after their game against the Patriots, showing a Rams victory.

"Sorry, Nick." Alex rubbed his eyes. "What's up?"

"You, me, Landon, and Tanner are in group two," Nick smiled. "Let's grab a table."

"Hey, Alex." Landon folded his hands on the desk. "Is Greenbriar Day's defense tough?"

"Very man." Alex frowned. "You know how when paper towels in the bathroom lie in the toilets, it can't flush? That's what the Patriots do: clog our passing lanes."

After Mrs. Conway explained the lab instructions based on Bohr's atom model, Alex conversed with his group members. Suggesting they work on the element sodium, Alex charged Landon with identifying the atomic structure, Tanner to look up the element in their textbook, and Nick to draw the circle.

"So, we make quicker passes, right?" Landon's eyes were full of hope. "That way, we can catch them off guard, you know?"

"If they fall for it, man," Tanner insisted, flipping to the glossary. He was the same height and build as Alex with a bleached blond ivy-league haircut. "Otherwise, their defenders knock you down."

"Right," Alex nodded in agreement. "And Greenbriar Day hits their opponents hard."

Alex's classmate wasn't lying. Having played alongside Tanner until sixth grade, Alex could count the number of times on both hands that his childhood teammate got knocked down against their rivals. Alex remembered Tanner being carried off the field with assistance because of minor injuries. It always made Alex cringe when his classmate's head bounced off the grass, or his leg bent awkwardly after getting tangled up with an opponent.

Within a split second, Alex heard the click-clacking of high-heels against the tiled floor nearby. Looking up and eying his teacher walking around the classroom, checking on any progress, Alex felt his heartbeat double in speed at the amount of headway their group made.

Oh shoot, I'm in trouble now.

"Mr. Tomassini." Mrs. Conway stood in front of group 2's table. "Step outside with me for a moment."

"Yes, ma'am." Alex closed his eyes and imagined himself anywhere but at school. "I wasn't...

"NOW, Mr. Tomassini!" Mrs. Conway frowned, then raised her eyebrows. "I'd like to speak with you."

In unison, the entire class let out, "Oooo, Alex is in trouble!" in unison.

"None of that," Mrs. Conway's voice was stern. "Get back to work."

When Alex made his way to the hallway, he could only stare at the floor. Not understanding what he could've done wrong or what his teacher wanted, Alex shoved his hands into his pockets and leaned against a locker. He looked up at Mrs. Conway.

Maybe I'll receive a warning and not get sent to the dean.

"Now, Alex!" Mrs. Conway stared at her student. "You know my rules about off-topic conversations during class. While I'm aware of your big game coming up, you'll need to focus more on your schoolwork and less on soccer right now."

"I know." Alex pursed his lips, then frowned. "Landon is new to the team and everything. He had some questions about Greenbriar Day."

"I understand that, Mr. Tomassini." Mrs. Conway stole a look through the square glass cutout at her students and then turned to Alex. "Be that as it may, though, it's distracting to your classmates. Please save discussions unrelated to science class until later."

Gee whiz Mrs. Conway.

Alex took a deep breath in and exhaled. Not being one to lose his temper during class, Alex resisted the urge to talk back. It frustrated Alex that even though Mrs. Conway's son was on the team, she didn't understand Landon's anxiety or, worse, didn't care. Alex didn't care that he broke a classroom rule. He wanted to be there for his teammate.

School's hard enough on its own without teachers that play everything by the book. There were plenty of those.

Unlike his older brother, Alex had a terrible poker face. Beaumont Christian held a holiday concert in fifth grade with the entire class. After the show ended, Alex and one of his best buddies Spencer Donnelly, raced to their Language Arts classroom.

Claiming to have forgotten supplies, the boys entered the room and found a jar full of money sitting on Mrs. Ashburn's desk. Having both put money in over the last few weeks for saying anything except "yes" in response to a question, Spencer encouraged Alex to steal, to which he said, "No!" and stormed off. Later that evening, while at Fitzpatrick's Frozen Yogurt, Spencer offered to pay for his and Alex's treats. Spencer turned to Alex to validate his scheme with a wink, trading words with his mom about where the funds had come. Alex told Mrs. Donnelly, "Spencer stole the money from the class jar."

Alex not only lost his buddy that night, but Spencer transferred to Greenbriar Day and now considered him a rival.

"Fine, Mrs. Conway." Alex sighed as his shoulders dropped. "I was only trying to help out a teammate.

"Is there something wrong, Alex?" Mrs. Conway raised an eyebrow. "You're acting so standoffish."

Where do I start? Even though the Rams were undefeated, they weren't united.

A big reason for that was player roles changing and nobody being on board. Landon was still adjusting to his new position and pleasing Coach Schallhorn while also facing his son Kellen's pressure. As for Connor, Alex noticed him becoming more distant and irritable since he left his house Sunday. It shouldn't have surprised Mrs. Conway that Alex had trouble concentrating on classwork with everything outside of class.

"Everything's fine." Alex rubbed his temples. "I'm a little tired, is all."

"You're one of my best students, Alex." Mrs. Conway lowered her voice. "Don't hesitate to tell me if you're having a bad day and need someone to chat with. I expect great things from you."

Science class seemed ominous to Alex when he reentered the classroom. Settling back into the seat next to Nick and crossing his arms, Alex tried to refocus.

Mrs. Conway didn't have to call me out. Everybody in class has off-topic conversations.

"I didn't get you in trouble," Landon glanced at his classmate. "Did I, Alex?"

#

Alex caught the basketball with both hands at the top of the key inside one of two gymnasiums inside Vitiello Athletic Center. Dribbling right and eying a classmate setting a screen nearby, Alex rolled off and then hauled a pass to Phil in the left corner. He loved when they played basketball in Phys ed class.

Watching his best friend taking on an opponent of similar size, Alex raced close by as Connor trailed behind. He tingled with excitement whenever he traded his school uniform for gym gear, and it was a nice break from lectures and worksheets. Alex wondered if Phil was as concerned about Connor losing his cool as he was.

"Let's go." Alex clapped his hands. "Shoot or pass it."

While studying Phil sprinting toward the hoop, Alex spotted Connor flashing past and heading in the same direction. Remembering his best friend preferred lay-ups over jump shots if he had the opportunity, Alex considered Phil a daredevil who never shied away from contact. Even though it was a pickup game, Alex worried that his classmate might hurt himself.

Alex surveyed Phil's leap and extended his arm as Connor slammed into him at that exact moment.

The ball hovered in the air before dropping through the net. Connor grabbed the rebound.

Excellent finish, buddy.

Alex twisted his face in disgust when his best friend landed hard on his right side outside the baseline. Alex rushed over. Kneeling beside Phil and studying him, Alex helped his classmate sit and eventually get back to his feet.

"What the heck, Connor?" Phil held a hand over his hip and leg as he limped toward his classmate. "It's gym class, not tryouts."

"That's for taking coach's side," Connor said, stuffing the basketball into Phil's stomach. "Maybe now you'll stop running your mouth."

"Forget you!" Phil gasped. "Don't blame me because you've sucked at soccer recently and lost your spot."

"Say that again!" Connor glared at his teammate. "I dare you."

Classmates' heads turned as Alex stepped between his pals and extended his arms to separate them.

"Back off, Connor." Alex curled his lip. "Stop picking on Phil."

"Or what, Alex?" Connor turned his chin up. "you'll tell the teacher. Let Phil stand up for himself."

Whatever, man.

Alex took his place on the foul line and traded the ball back and forth on a checkup with Connor. Alex stretched his arms out to the sides with bent knees and chested up in a defensive stance.

"Let's go, King Con," Alex waved his arms in front of his taller classmate. "Bring it on."

As a defender, Alex knew the importance of staying low and shortening his sliding steps. He hustled around with him and matched every stride. Partnering with Phil on a double team near the right sideline, Alex put his hand above the ball. Alex stared at his classmate, swiping the ball away, stumbling out of bounds.

"Yeah, Alex," Phil called out from nearby. "Great, D!"

Dribbling near half-court to clear the ball, Alex gazed at open classmates. He faked a pass left before lunging across the foul line seeing Phil in the right-hand corner. Lifting his arm for a layup, Alex forged a shot and flicked a pass in his best friend's direction.

"Take the shot, Phil." Alex backpedaled five steps back behind the three-point line. "You've got it, buddy!"

Phil launched a shot, snatching the pass and squaring his body toward the basket.

The ball glided toward the basketball before dropping through the net.

"Yes!" Alex raced toward Phil and chest bumped him. "That's game."

Checking his fallen teammate out, Alex trotted toward Connor. He hoped Connor was okay. Finding Connor sitting against bleachers, Alex gave his friend a once-over. Frowning at how red Connor's face was and how he kept leaning forward, Alex didn't understand why his classmate treated Phys Ed like his life depended on it.

"Hey." Alex offered a hand. "Are you alright?"

"What do you care?" Connor swatted away Alex's hand. "You and Phil left me here and kept on playing."

"Sorry, dude." Alex cracked. "We were in the middle of a game."

"Wait till team workouts," Connor pushed himself to his feet. "You'll be sorry!"

Alex felt the familiar tightening of his chest. Alex worried about not knowing what he meant by the threat or if Connor would carry it out. He'd thought being there for his teammate on Sunday was enough.

What does Connor mean?

Chapter Eight
Tangled with Torment

Alex surveyed from the right touchline as Coach Schallhorn rolled a ball out to a pair of teammates in red pinnies outside the center circle on Beaumont Christian's soccer field during Wednesday afternoon's team workout.

"Hey Alex," Phil said, raising a knee toward his chest. "Did you finish the discussion questions for The Outsiders yet?"

"Yeah." Alex studied two boys he recognized as reserves trading the ball between them and crossing the center mark. "Chapters three and four are the hardest so far."

Alex was familiar with the drill. Before trying out for the school's team, he played for Greenbriar United Soccer Association, and his coach ran it. Loving the up-tempo style because it mimicked an intensity only found during game scenarios, Alex found himself in much better shape. At first, it wasn't easy when his dad enrolled him in speed and agility sessions; Alex complained of tight legs at every turn. Remembering S.J. told him Coach Schallhorn's workouts were long and grueling a year before entering middle school, Alex invited Phil along to work on conditioning and stamina exercises as much as they could.

Maybe I could be like S.J. Or at least half of what he is.

"No kidding, man." Phil's eyes widened. "I stayed up until midnight finishing them."

Alex turned back to the field. Spotting a shorter boy feint past a defender wearing a white pinny who happened to be a reserve, then boot the pass toward his teammate, Alex smiled at how in sync they were. Lunging forward with his right leg and then dropping to a knee, Alex rested his hands on his leg and leaned forward.

It was midway through a slow and lousy week. First, Alex was marked tardy twice in school and narrowly avoided earning detention. If that wasn't bad enough, focusing on various assignments proved almost impossible for Alex, resulting in flunked quizzes for Science and Math classes. And then there was Connor.

"Next up!" Coach Schallhorn stood opposite the touchline as the boys exchanged low fives as a new pair trotted onto the field.

The whistle blew.

Following two starter teammates retrieving a pass outside the north penalty box, Alex recognized both boys on offense.

No way Coach Schallhorn suggested Kellen and Connor partner up for any drill, above all this one.

Staring at Connor with a stink-eye, Alex could think about gym class and swallowed a lump in his throat. While lunging forward with the opposite leg and resting hands on his knee, Alex winced at the emerging tightness.

It wasn't only his hips and legs that were tight. Everything hurts.

"Hey Alex," Phil pushed his best friend further. "You know what's going to happen, right?"

"What's that, Phil?" Alex winced as he pushed himself to his feet. "Connor and Kellen one-upping each other."

"Exactly, man," Phil told Alex. "And one of them will make a bad pass and make it harder for the other to score."

"Or worse, get slide tackled." Alex shook his head. "Either way, it won't end well, bud."

Kellen crossed the center mark back on the field before sprinting past an opponent, dribbling into white pinny territory, and looking left at his teammate, matching strides. He exploded outside the south penalty box and eyed Connor waving his arm nearby.

"Why doesn't Kellen play on offense?" Phil's eyes gleamed. "He's super agile and a beast with his first touch."

"His dad won't let him." Alex snatched a water bottle from close by and chugged it. "Plus, Kellen would rather tackle and break up passes."

"That's what he's best at," Phil said, using his shirt sleeve to wipe sweat from his face. "Kellen's defense is a big reason we're still undefeated."

"Indeed, Phil." Alex pointed to the defender shadowing Connor. "If Kellen does a cross pass now, Connor might score."

Kellen continued a dazzling display of dribbling until he heard shouts almost as if on cue. Glancing over at Connor, still racing around with minimal space between him and an opponent, Kellen scoffed at his teammate.

"Quit being a ball hog, Kellen," Connor said, gritting his teeth. "Pass it to me already."

"Fine, Snodgrass." Kellen lofted a pass toward his teammate in mid-stride. "But you'd better score."

What good is it to run this drill if nobody passes when they're supposed to?

Back on the touchlines, Alex stomped his foot. When he recognized the opponent covering Landon, Alex resisted the urge to smile. The last thing Alex wanted to do was show favoritism, never so during a drill.

"What's he doing?" Phil crossed his arms. "Kellen wasted way too much time passing."

"Showing off." Alex shook his head. "He's trying to make Connor mess up."

Connor took the pass off his cleat near the touchlines on the field. As he turned and bumped shoulders with Landon, Connor snarled and lunged forward. Charging into the penalty box and setting his sights on the goal, Connor sensed a sharp pain while lifting his leg. As he fired a shot, someone slammed into Connor.

The ball veered right and soared above the net and out of play, cruising toward the goal.

"What gives, Snodgrass?" Kellen hurried over and inspected his teammate. "You're awful at shooting."

"Don't blame me, Kellen," Connor sat on the ground with his hands around his knees. "I hardly get any reps anymore, thanks to your dad taking my spot away."

Watching the interaction between his teammates made Alex cringe. He couldn't tell if or when Connor might blow up. Knowing how the coach's son felt about their teammate and how he wanted him off the team, Alex wasn't surprised when Kellen stepped over Connor and helped Landon to his feet. For now, though, all Alex could do was hope his teammates wouldn't fight.

"After what I saw, that was the right move," Kellen cracked. "You've stunk on the field since the season started."

"Forget you, Kellen," Connor said, springing to his feet and facing off with his teammate. "Not everybody's as perfect as you."

"You've got that right, Connor." Kellen set his hands on his hips. "It must be hard being such a loser."

Walk away, Connor.

Understanding he was only trying to defend his pride from the embarrassment of being scored on didn't make Alex feel more comfortable. It was apparent that something was going down. Not wanting to get between the teammates and be forced to choose sides, Alex remained on the touchlines. He thought *we've got the Greenbriar game in a few days*, surveying a group of teammates surrounding the pair.

Are these two butting heads causing issues with the whole team?

"What did you call me, Schallhorn?" Connor's lip curled.

"Are you deaf?" Kellen shoved his teammate. "You're a loser!"

The whistle blew as Coach Schallhorn stepped between the boys. Sticking his arms out like a baseball umpire signaling "safe," the coach blocked his players from going at each other as teammates jumped in to intervene.

"Cheese and crackers, boys," Coach Schallhorn folded his arms. "I have zero tolerance for fighting on this team."

"Kellen started it," Connor said, throwing his arms up. "He was being a showboating ball hog and passed late on purpose."

"You're such a liar, Snobgrass," Kellen sneered. "You can't stand that I'm a better athlete, and someone took your spot."

"A newbie," Connor argued. "Who you probably told daddy to replace me in the lineup with, you spoiled brat."

"Enough, boys!" Coach Schallhorn's face was redder than a brick. "Any more lip from either of you or the team earns additional torture runs."

The rest of the team let out a collective groan followed by shouts of arguments directed toward the boys.

Twenty minutes later, the Ram players gathered around the center circle for cool-down stretching led by Kellen. Before joining their teammates, Alex spotted Connor still fuming from his earlier incident and waved him over.

"Hey, Connor." Alex felt out of breath. "If we expect to keep winning, you'll have to start putting the team first."

"Putting the team first?" Connor turned his chin up. "I show up at every workout and training session coach holds, even on days I have baseball. I don't know what you're talking about."

"Sure, yeah," Alex's gaze bounced between his teammates midway through leg stretches and Connor, "when you're here. But lately, you've been on another planet. You're constantly exhausted on the field. You can't focus and concentrate when it's time to. Never mind your fits of rage when things don't go your way. Then today, you're mouthing off to coach and picking fights with teammates."

"Hey, Kellen started that with a bad pass," Connor said, crossing his arms and frowning. "Not my fault the coach's son hates my guts. Maybe you should get on him for pointing the finger at everyone else instead of himself."

"You responded then played your victim card." Alex sighed. "You were looking for a fight. That's not being the better teammate."

"Better teammate?" Connor glared at Alex and scoffed. "How can I do that when everybody rides me all the time? I'm doing the best I can here, and it's never good enough."

"Nobody wants anything except your best," Alex folded his arms across his chest. "That's all anyone can ask of you or anyone else on this team. If that's too much for you to handle, you shouldn't be here."

"Maybe not," Connor glared at his teammate. "But you don't deserve to be captain either. Nobody who talks to teammates, much less friends like that, is a leader."

"Who said we're still friends?" Alex's heart pounded. "Our friendship ended when you stabbed Phil and me in the back during Phys Ed."

"Is that so?" Connor's voice quivered. "Well, you're no different than every stuffed shirt that goes to school here."

"Real classy, buddy." Alex blushed. "Just go home and let the real players finish workouts."

Alex turned around and then repeatedly shook his head. He wasn't sure whether ending the friendship hurt him or Connor more. *Being friends with Connor is like riding a roller coaster.* While hustling toward the center circle, Alex saw teammates pairing up for their final stretches and hung his head.

Suddenly, Alex heard a nearby voice yell, "I told you earlier, you'd be sorry!" then, without delay, he crashed onto the halfway line. Landing hard on his right side and grabbing his leg, Alex looked up to find some teammates standing before him and others holding Connor back.

Taking Phil and Landon's hands, he rose to his feet. Alex could only stare at his former friend sauntering toward the locker room at Finley's fieldhouse. Connor paused and turned before putting the final nail in the coffin.

"Forgot you, jerks," Connor hollered, his eyes watered. "I quit!"

#

"You haven't touched your sandwich," S.J. said, glancing at his younger brother's plate. "I know it hurts. What happened with Connor, but refusing to eat isn't the answer."

"Then what is?" Alex huddled his arms over the table. "Not only did we lose a teammate before the Greenbriar game, but I also lost a close friend."

"That you did everything to try and help," S.J. reassured. "Yet Connor blindsided you while walking back to stretch. You've got nothing to feel bad about, Alex."

"Why do I?" Alex swigged some iced water.

Forty-five minutes after workouts ended, Alex sat next to S.J. at a circular table inside Clontz's café, ignoring his older brother's efforts to lift his spirits. Alex had taken up S.J.'s offer to go somewhere to talk after climbing into the Ridgeline outside the locker room at Finley's Fieldhouse. Spending most of the ride crossing his arms and avoiding eye contact, Alex wasn't in the mood to rehash today's events. If only he could enroll at a boarding school for the rest of the school year, Alex might be able to steer clear of embarrassment. He wanted to skip school tomorrow and for the rest of the week.

Now taking a bite of a turkey sandwich, Alex ran his mind back through workouts. Trying to figure out where everything had gone wrong and coming up empty only hurt Alex's head. He wondered if something had happened with his former friend between Sunday and today. Noticing they'd talked less and less ever since he left, Alex suspected more was going on than he ever knew. If anything was ever more explicit, Alex needed more than ever at this moment. It was somebody to lean on.

"You've been friends since elementary school," S.J. said, scrolling through his phone. "It's not easy to let go of a bond you've had for that long. Middle school isn't a piece of cake even if you're popular, believe me, little brother."

"Yeah, right, S.J." Alex stuck his tongue out and blew. "I bet you ruled the hallways at Beaumont Christian."

"Most of the time, yes." S.J. nodded. "But that didn't mean I wasn't a target for peer pressure."

"No way!" Alex almost choked on his sandwich. "Like what?"

"Smoking and drinking at the very least," S.J.'s eyes widened. "We cheated off each other's tests and excluded others if they didn't think like us."

Alex didn't know this side of S.J. As far as Alex knew, his older brother was the favorite son who couldn't do anything wrong. It surprised Alex that S.J. had flaws and wasn't the perfect model of a video game character everyone viewed him as. Not that he'd root against his older brother: Alex understood there were different standards between them.

"Wow, man." Alex blinked. "I never knew about any of that."

"You wouldn't have," S.J. admitted. "Because dad handled everything, I never got in trouble through school. Dad punished me privately."

Alex stayed silent. Not even asking for details, he understood what his older brother meant. Their dad was famous for scolding others on Capitol Hill when deemed necessary, and as Alex experienced, it wasn't any different at home. Alex thought he and his brother had the strictest father ever.

"Speaking of dad." Alex changed the subject. "Is he coming to the Greenbriar game?"

"Yes, Alex." S.J. smiled. "He'll be there."

"Awesome." Alex swallowed the remains of his sandwich. "I want to make him proud."

"Of course, bud," S.J. said, resting a hand on Alex's shoulder. "But don't overdo it. A lot of games left to play."

Alex nodded. There was nothing more important to Alex than winning and impressing his dad. Acknowledging his older brother's point about not overdoing it since many games remained, Alex took the advance with a grain of salt. Expected always to give 110% no matter what by his coach, Alex didn't like that he was ridden harder than anyone else on the team.

Please, God, allow me to play the best I'm capable of.

Chapter Nine
Rematch Revisited

Alex galloped across the center mark of Greenbriar Day School's soccer field. Dribbling into Patriots territory and straightaway met by a sea of royal blue jerseys, he bumped shoulders with a pair of defenders who shoved him hard. Lofting a pass in Phil's direction before falling over, Alex landed with force on his stomach. "All part of the game," he told himself.

It was two days later Friday when Beaumont Christian and Greenbriar Day met in last season's Pac-7 conference championship rematch. The two teams appeared to pick up right where they'd left off, with both teams trading possessions back and forth. A glance toward the scoreboard revealed a tied game. Neither team appeared to give an inch, continuously committing fouls, and being shown yellow cards. Much physicality seemed evident as sweat dripped off bodies, legs clashed before getting tangled up, and whistles shrilled through the hot early September afternoon.

Alex managed to get himself onto a knee and push himself up to his feet. As he looked up to survey how the play progressed, Alex couldn't help but smile at his team pushing further into Greenbriar territory. While dashing forward to catch up, he caught a glimpse of his father in the stands.

I can't be any less than perfect. Dad wouldn't accept that.

"Hey Alex," Landon said, struggling to fight off multiple opponents. "A little help!"

"Right behind, dude." Alex sprinted to the right outside the center circle with a defender following close by. "Pass it here, quick!"

Just as Landon sent the ball to him, Spencer Donnelly, the boy who marked Alex since the game began, stepped in front, and robbed his pass. Bending his knees and bumping shoulders with his opponent, Alex continued jockeying for possession while staying on his toes.

What the!

"Get off, Tomassini!" Spencer shoved Alex. "You can't stop me."

"Shut up, Donnelly." Alex poked his foot between his opponent and the ball. "You're nothing!"

Spencer was half an inch taller than Alex with a sturdy build. He had short brown hair with beady blue eyes. As the attacking midfielder for Greenbriar Day, Spencer's combination of power and speed made him a force to be reckoned with.

Alex grunted as he fought for possession inside Ram territory. Clutching Spencer's sliver-gray shorts and pulling them without cease, Alex snuck a cleat in, then booted the ball away. Both boys crashed to the ground without delay and landed hard on their sides, struggling to recover.

Gripping his leg and gingerly turning over, Alex stared at the clear blue skies above. A throbbing pain alarmed him as he ran a hand from the back of his leg toward his knee. Taking a pair of offered hands from teammates, Alex limped around and tried walking it off.

Please be a cramp. Please be a cramp.

Meanwhile, the ball sailed toward the net and then bounced. Egan caught it with both hands. Evaluating the field and taking a few steps outside the goalie box, Egan punted the ball high in the air.

Ram and Patriot players exploded at the center circle in the air, vying for the incoming ball. Both Phil and Landon collided with teammates and opponents, contending for possession. Squeezing between numerous white jerseys, Phil tried heading the ball toward teammates, but a taller and broad-shouldered Patriot arrived just a millisecond faster.

Alex turned and found Spencer still lying on his side outside the Rams penalty box. Hobbling over to help him up, Alex smiled when his opponent recovered and sat up with arms draped over his knees. At first, Alex wasn't sure how receptive his childhood buddy would be to sportsmanship but figured he'd try. Leaning over and offering a hand, Alex's heartbeat doubled in speed when his opponent shot him a hostile glare.

"What the heck, Alex?" Spencer swatted the Rams captain's hand away. "I don't need help up, definitely not from you."

"Sorry, Spence." Alex curled a lip. "I thought you were hurt; I was only trying to help."

Almost instantaneously, Alex heard Coach Schallhorn hollering from the away touchlines.

"C'mon, Rams," Coach Schallhorn folded his arms. "Focus on the game."

On that occasion, inside Ram territory, another Patriot midfielder, Trevor Nachman, gathered the ball off his chest and let it drop to his feet near the right touchline. At the same time, he feinted past a pair of Ram defenders and Landon, who'd recovered. Trevor inched near the penalty box and was stopped mid-stride by Kellen. As the two boys of similar size battled for possession, Spencer emerged.

Trevor was taller and thicker. He had short strawberry blond hair with messy spikes and warm brown eyes. Being the fastest player on Greenbriar Day, Trevor threatened with his swiftness.

"Let's go, Landon," Alex said, observing his teammate pairing up on a double team with Kellen. "Get the ball out of there. You've got this."

At that moment, Alex tracked Spencer advancing toward the penalty box. Without hesitation, he raced toward his opponent on an angle with the hope of halting Greenbriar's midfielder. Alex lunged forward and planted his foot near Spencer when his leg tightened up. Bumping his opponent with more force than he had all game, Alex grunted as he tried bringing Spencer down.

Within a split second, Alex faced his most challenging dilemma of the game. Deciding whether to illegally tackle his opponent and earn a yellow card for preventing a goal or prying the ball free made Alex think back to a lesson in religion class about sacrifice. The lesson centered around John 15:13 about laying down one's life for friends. Once Spencer lifted his leg, Alex ducked underneath and fired the ball to Kellen.

Although both had stumbled to the grass, adrenaline kicked into high gear as Alex sprung to his feet first. Gathering in a pass from Kellen as he crossed the center mark, Alex glided past several opponents and approached Patriot territory. As he looked around for an open teammate, Alex found Phil wide open on the left and Landon sprinting along the right sideline.

"Over here, Alex," Phil said, flashing around and getting his teammate's attention. "Pass me the ball, bud."

"I got you, Alex." Landon turned back and waved. "Send the ball my way."

Alex spotted Spencer lunging in his direction before booting a pass out of the corner of his eye.

Phil trapped the ball between his legs before dropping it to his feet. Working against multiple Patriot players, Alex squeezed between two defenders who came together for a double-team. Sending a cross pass to Landon earned him the worst knockdown of the afternoon thus far. Phil stared as his teammate took the ball in stride, then booted it to Nick, who struck the ball in a millisecond just as animatedly as it arrived. Yet this wasn't enough as the Greenbriar goalie came up with a save. Beaumont Christian fans shook their heads in disbelief in the stands, but something else caught the boy's attention: their captain was down.

Alex lay curled up on his side. Clutching his upper leg and slapping the ground with his hand, Alex cried out in pain. Feeling like he'd finished an ironman match in a WWE video game, Alex wondered if he'd be able to walk off the field without help.

As he draped his arms around his teammates' shoulders and was carried toward the locker room, Alex caught a glimpse of his dad in the stands. He observed the despondent expression stretched across his face, tightening his chest. Even knowing there was no way he could let anyone in his family down, much less his dad. It only fired Alex up.

It doesn't matter if I'm on one leg. I've got to be on the field.

# #

Alex grimaced as he gathered a pass from Egan off his thigh outside Beaumont Christian's penalty box early in the second half. Not unexpectedly, the hamstring injury suffered earlier had hampered his mobility, but Alex wasn't using this fact as an excuse. Being trapped inside his head was much worse for Alex than aches and pains. "Quit acting like a wimp," he imagined his dad saying. "It's only a sore hammy. Even S.J.'s played through worse. I didn't raise you to be a quitter."

Flashing across the center mark, countless Patriot defenders surrounded Alex. He faked left and slashed right, which caught several opponents off-guard. Advancing out of the center circle and bumping shoulders with a pair of defenders, one of which was Spencer, Alex desperately searched for an open teammate as a sharp pain emerged in his leg.

"Over here, Alex," Landon said, hustling around Greenbriar territory in the proximity of his teammate. "I'm open, dude."

Wincing at cleats striking his legs, Alex lofted a pass in Landon's direction before crashing to the ground prone. As his leg seized up, Alex pounded the ground.

Owww! I don't know how much more I can handle.

"How does that grass taste, Alex?" Spencer smirked, then stepped over his opponent. "There's more where that came from if you don't leave the game."

"Keep talking, Spence." Alex looked up at his nemesis. "I'll get you back soon enough."

Inside Greenbriar territory, Alex pushed himself up to both knees. Forcing himself to his feet and surveying the action, he kneaded the back of his leg and winced. Alex was impressed by how well his teammates were playing. It was noticeable enough to Alex that their opponents gave the Rams everything they had.

Dashing around Greenbriar territory the best he could, Alex stared at his best friend, lifting his leg, and firing a shot on goal. Rooting for his team to score and lead by one, Alex remained nearby if a possession changed.

The ball rocketed toward the goal and veered right. The Greenbriar goalie leaped and tipped it with both hands. A whistle blew as the ball landed behind the net and out of play.

"Jiminy Christmas!" Phil slapped his hands together. "Why can't I score today?"

Alex greeted Phil near the touchline. Curling an arm around his teammate's shoulders, Alex pulled him closer.

"Don't sweat it, bro." Alex encouraged. "We'll beat them on the corner kick, no worries."

"Yeah, dude," Phil frowned. "I wanted that goal."

The whistle blew again.

"Corner kick, white!" The referee motioned to the Rams.

Alex raced to the right penalty marker. Studying his teammates lined up in a train pattern, he took a few steps away from the ball and aimed his kick. Firing the shot outside the Patriots goalie box, Alex hurried into action.

Landon exploded from his spot in the pattern. Pushing off his right foot and fixing his eyes on the ball, he locked his ankle before flicking a shot toward the bottom left side of the net.

The ball bounced toward the left side of the goal. He hustled toward the fast-approaching sphere; the Patriots goalie dove in front of it. Landing hard on his left shoulder, the Patriots goalie caught the ball.

Come on, man, can't we put the ball in the goal? Alex thought as he watched the Greenbriar Day goalie punt the ball back into play.

Alex bolted around Greenbriar territory. He raked fingers through his hair and sighed. The more time spent chasing down the ball and getting knocked down, the worse the throbbing in Alex's hamstring became.

Nothing better than rivalry games. Everybody leaves everything they've got on the field.

The whistle blew.

"Man, that Greenbriar goalie is tough," Landon wiped his sweaty head with a forearm. "I've never missed that shot."

"Until now, right?" Alex cracked. "Welcome to the Pac-7, man."

"The competition is fierce, Alex." Landon made a goofy face. "Think we'll go into overtime?"

"Your hammy still bothering you?" Landon gave the Rams captain a once-over. "You should sub out and stretch."

"No way, Landon," Alex responded. "Not an option."

The whistle blew and interrupted Alex's conversation and thoughts.

"Time out, white!" The referee gestured to the left touchline.

"Not an option?" Landon's eyes widened. "You'd better rest, dude, before you push yourself too hard."

That won't happen." Alex wasn't upset by his teammate's remarks. Knowing from growing up in a sports-obsessed family where being second-best wasn't acceptable, Alex couldn't help himself.

Nothing else matters when the whistle blows except winning.

The Rams and Patriots traded the ball back and forth for another fifteen minutes. Fatigue set in as muscles cramped and routines move on the field second-guessed.

Fans of both teams remained on their feet, trying to rally their squads on.

Neither team capitalized on possessions until the five-minute mark. Greenbriar Day took a 4-2 lead. It was open season on Egan as the Patriot's offensive attack scored goals at will. Spencer and Trevor both scored goals as their opponents could only look on. Nick and the other Ram forward, Xavier, exchanged passes on the kickoff. Nick tapped the ball behind before he and Xavier hustled into Greenbriar territory.

Alex took the ball off his knee. Dribbling across the center mark and right off, met by Spencer. Hearing his opponent's labored breathing as they brushed shoulders, Alex flashed into Patriot's territory and searched for an open teammate.

I've got to get away from Spencer. Otherwise, I won't have a chance to score.

"Still on the field, Alex?" Spencer stuck Alex above the shin guard while ramming his shoulder into his opponent with force. "I figured you'd be on the sidelines by now."

"Keep taking cheap shots, Donnelly." Alex's heart pounded as he pulled on Spencer's jersey. "See what happens, man."

"Or what, Tomassini?" Spencer refused to let up and stayed on Alex like butter on toast. "you'll tell the referee on me as you ratted to my mom in fifth grade? It doesn't work that way, Alex."

In an instant, Phil broke free of his opponent and darted to the left corner. Waving his hand and trying to draw his best friend's attention, Phil appeared to have a second wind.

"Over here, bud," Phil remained one step ahead of his opponent, who attempted to match strides. "I'm open, Alex!"

Alex advanced the ball toward Greenbriar's penalty arc. Setting the sole of his right cleat and faking left, Alex slashed right into the penalty box. Backpedaling and rolling the ball up, Alex executed a stutter-step move.

It looked fantastic, but he also thought, grinning as his opponent crumbled to the grass. *It got spencer off my back.*

Almost breathlessly, Alex saw Patriot defenders swarming nearby. He felt his chest tighten as time ran out. Lifting his leg and firing a shot toward the goal, Alex felt opponents barreling into him from all sides. Crumbling to the ground and bouncing off his side, Alex covered his eyes as he writhed in pain.

The ball whizzed toward the goal. The Patriot goalie smacked the ball away as it bounced into Greenbriar territory, where the Rams and the Patriots battled for possession.

In the meantime, Landon darted toward the crowds and opponents. Landon tried and successfully pried the ball free by squeezing between a pair of Patriot center backs. Eying Phil kneeling beside the fallen Rams captain, Landon frowned but continued striking the ball. Landon booted a shot toward the goal by dribbling into Greenbriar's penalty box and pulling the ball back.

The whistle blew as Ram players hung their heads.

Inside the penalty box, Alex was still down and in pain. Uncovering his eyes and looking up at his best friend beside him, Alex twisted his face in disgust. Trying to narrow down what hurt most, Alex didn't know where to start.

I can't bail. We must beat Greenbriar.

"That's enough, buddy," Phil lay a hand on his teammate's shoulder. "You've got to see Vance now. I can't stand seeing you in pain anymore."

"No way." Alex shook his head even as tears streamed down his face. "I'm not giving up on you guys."

"Dude!" Phil scoffed, giving his best friend an exasperated glare. "I don't care what you say. You're going to the touchlines."

While being helped to his feet, Alex stole a look at the scoreboard and shook his head. He couldn't believe the rematch of last year's championship game would end with him unable to finish the game. Settling under teammates' shoulders and only staring at the ground, Alex heard fans of both sides applaud as his feet glided across the grass.

Gosh, darn it!

Alex planted himself onto a trainer's table behind the Rams bench. With under three minutes to play, Coach Schallhorn decided Alex couldn't play the rest of the afternoon. A Beaumont Christian athletic trainer's evaluation determined that Alex had pulled his hamstring, which would sideline him for at least two weeks.

Dad must think I'm a disappointment. I let him and everyone else down.

Chapter Ten
Facing the Fallout

It was around an hour later that same day when Alex sat in the backseat of his dad's dark-colored SUV in between S.J and Vincent, nibbling his fingernails. He hadn't bothered changing out of his uniform after the team bus made the short ride back from Greenbriar Day School, and nobody questioned it either. A treatment plan for his injured hamstring was about as long as a CVS receipt and didn't exactly leave Alex very encouraged. It made him feel even worse.

Dad's grilling is the only thing more awful than nursing an injury.

"What were you thinking, son?" Mr. Tomassini said, his gaze bouncing between the rearview mirror and the road. "You know how important it is to stretch and stay healthy?

"I know, Dad." Alex winced as he adjusted himself in the seat. "But I couldn't let my team down."

"You already have," Mr. Tomassini gripped the leather-stitched steering wheel tightly. "By not getting treatment when you had a chance and continuing to play."

"Yeah, well." Alex felt his heart pounding. "I don't know what you expect me to do."

"Quit acting so gosh darn selfish," Mr. Tomassini raised his voice. "You need to learn when to put your health before your ego."

Alex crossed his arms. He wasn't sure whether to shout back or stay silent. Looking at S.J. to the left and Vincent to the right, who both wore the same expression, made Alex question if he even deserved to wear the Ram uniform.

Dad makes everyone feel awful if they're anything less than perfect.

"What ego?" Alex threw his arms up. "I'm like the best player on the team and not to mention the captain, so I've got to be out there no matter what."

"Which is why you're sidelined," Mr. Tomassini rolled the car to a stop at a red light and turned. "And until you understand that you can't control everything that happens on the field, you'll continue taking unnecessary risks and get hurt."

"Sal, sweetheart," Mrs. Tomassini rested a hand on her husband's shoulder. "You don't need to be that hard on him."

"Seriously, Dad," S.J. curled an arm around Alex's shoulder. "Ease up on Alex. He played his heart out today."

Alex hung his head. He couldn't grasp why his dad didn't appreciate his efforts on the field and everything he did well. Realizing that the next two weeks would be harder than ever made Alex admit he needed support.

It's going to suck not being able to play.

Alex ran a hand underneath his leg and frowned. He sensed the same ache that plagued him through the game. Unsure of how he'd even make it upstairs to his bedroom forced Alex to contemplate what mattered right now.

Maybe I'll come back and be better than ever, but what if I don't?

As his dad parked the car in the Tomassini family's garage and killed the ignition, Alex unbuckled his seatbelt. He moved right toward the opened door that Vincent had just stepped out of and paused. While giving his dad a stink eye before climbing, he knew things would worsen before they improved.

Instead of ripping all my shortfalls, I wish Dad focused on building off what I did well.

"Hey, Vincent." Alex made his way out of the SUV. "Can you help me upstairs?"

#

Alex's leg ached every time he moved and adjusted himself on his bed. He finally settled against some pillows, and channel surfed, knowing nothing on TV would help distract him right now. Recalling everything his dad said verbatim, almost like a scary horror movie, made it more difficult for Alex to think about anything else.

I'd rather be anywhere else than sitting at home.

What troubled Alex more than anything now was how others would perceive him from now on. He knew his teammates and friends, at least, wouldn't view him any differently, maybe as stubborn. Still, he could handle that as he considered the possibility of Coach Schallhorn deeming him injury-prone even after recovering made Alex feel nauseous.

I can only imagine how Dad would flip if I lost my starting spot permanently.

A knock on the door drew Alex away from his thoughts.

"It's me," S.J. called from outside, holding extra pillows and an ice pack. "Can I come in?"

"Yeah, sure." Alex turned his head and managed a slight smile.

"Thanks, bro," S.J. entered and set pillows on the bed before handing Alex the ice pack. "I wanted to check on you and see if you're alright."

"Yeah, thanks!" Alex stretched his legs out in front of him, making him grimace. "If you erase the game and car ride from my mind like they do in those Men in Black movies, I'd be even better."

Alex appreciated his older brother making sure he was okay. He wasn't sure how much chatting might help. Feeling like he'd just lost his identity as a soccer star made Alex more unsure of himself than before.

Will everybody still notice me, or am I just another kid in the hallways?

"I wish I could, buddy," S.J. planted himself on the side of his brother's bed. "But then everything you accomplish later on wouldn't mean much."

"Maybe not." Alex shrugged. "At least I wouldn't feel so terrible now."

"Come on, Alex," S.J. patted Alex's knee. "Don't let dad's scolding get you down."

"Easier said than done." Alex raised his leg halfway up but let it fall. "I don't know what hurts more, my leg or self-confidence."

Alex recognized where S.J. was going. He didn't even disagree with the sentiment. Feeling like he was inside the long and dark Pequabuck Tunnel forced Alex to consider if or when he'd find his way out.

I know things could worsen, but it doesn't make anything stink less right now.

"Your self-confidence most likely," S.J. studied his younger brother. "Since your hammy will heal in a few weeks."

"Not soon enough, though." Alex curled a lip. "I'm not looking forward to it at all."

"Think of it this way," S.J. cleared his throat, "now you have a chance to do service hours and get back in shape."

"Yeah, I guess." Alex gazed at his older brother. "It wouldn't be the worst use of time to help others."

Even as much as Alex hated to admit it, getting injured wasn't all bad. Sure, he'd miss games and workouts, but he needed a break. Having played on the all-stars little league over the summer before immediately starting soccer season left Alex with minimal time to recover.

Mom always used to tell us: that everything happens for a reason.

Chapter Eleven
Injury Itinerary

Alex felt his heart pounding as he bent his knee and stepped outward. He kept his hips back before releasing the position and pushing off his left foot. Hurtling across Beaumont Christian's fitness center and sensing his sore hamstring burning made Alex wonder when Vance might halt the exercises.

I'm nowhere near ready to hit the field yet, but I can train some.

Gazing ahead and seeing Vance standing at the front of the area, Alex wanted to prove to the athletic trainer that he meant business. Even being sidelined for ten to fourteen days, he needed to be committed to returning. Realizing that everything was much more significant than soccer and being on the field, Alex had to prove to his dad once and for all he could be the son he needed to be.

Could he step up when it mattered?

It had been five days since Alex got hurt during the rivalry game on Greenbriar day's field, and he wasted no time continuing his treatment plan on Tuesday afternoon. He spent the first few days riding a stationary bike before strengthening his hamstring and surrounding muscles with an ankle weight. Finishing those lighter sessions with exercise ball movements for balance, core, and leg strength before icing and elevating his leg in the training room encouraged Alex.

The last two days, he thought, *have been much more challenging.*

"Great job Alex," Vance said, extending a closed fist out to the Rams captain approaching him. "You're making great progress. How do you feel?"

"Tired!" Alex bumped Vance's fist and interlocked his hands around his head to catch his breath. "And my hammy burns."

"That's normal, buddy," Vance checked out Alex's gait and pressed his lips. "Go grab some water before we do some light passing drills."

"No more drills, Vance." Alex held up a hand and keeled over. "Please, my legs kill right now."

Alex wasn't lying. He'd been pushing himself fifty to seventy-five percent harder every day, and this session was no exception. Feeling like he'd have a setback if he didn't throw in the towel left Alex disappointed.

Vance expected a little more from me, and I know I let him down.

The self-doubt and shame continued plaguing Alex even as he limped toward the water fountain. He couldn't help but have sensations of worthlessness with his lack of progress. Expecting that he'd finish these sessions in full by now made Alex think he went one step forward and two steps back.

Alex returned to the fitness center to find Vance with his arms crossed. He gave the athletic trainer a once-over and noticed something different. Having worked closely with him recently, Alex knew what Vance expected.

I can't tell if he has bad news or not.

"Meet me in the training room," Vance made eye contact. "We'll finish with ice and some stretching."

#

"It's not your progress or effort that concerns me," Vance said, raising Alex's leg back. "It's the amount of tightness that you're feeling that's troubling."

"What do you mean?" Alex's voice cracked. "I thought you said earlier that the burning I felt was normal."

"After a grueling workout like yours, yes," Vance nodded. "But not the tension you have when I move your leg further."

"Right, yeah." Alex cringed. "But when can I get back on the field?"

Alex lay on a training table with his hands resting on his stomach, taking in everything the athletic trainer said a short while later. He'd done everything asked of him during these treatment sessions, well, almost. Complaining of tired legs just before the final drill of the day left Alex in a vulnerable spot.

It'll take even longer now before I can start working out with the team again.

The athletic training room was sizeable and swarming with activity. Some boys played various sports filed in and out for stretching, icing, evaluation, and more. Chattering, groaning, and occasional cries of pain overrode alternative rock music playing from a stereo nearby. The smell of antiseptic that spread through the area left athletes suppressing sneezes.

"Not until you can finish this session," Vance advanced Alex's leg near his head before bringing it across his body. "It matters because you'll have to do all that again in addition to jumping and sprints."

"Darn it." Alex threw his head back and then sighed. "So, I might be out even longer now?"

"Not much," Vance smiled. "You've got to understand that not everything happens when we want it."

Alex didn't respond. He realized taking more days was more important than rushing back. Having to rehab his injury for a few extra days irritated Alex, but he understood.

It's better to take extra time than rush back and risk injury.

As he turned onto his stomach for Vance to treat him further, Alex considered the chats with S.J. only days earlier. He realized that getting in shape was a top priority. Even as he sensed his leg be raised again then iced, Alex believed everything was worth the pain.

Chapter Twelve
Grappling with Guidance

AS Alex scooped a large spoonful of spaghetti and dropped a pile onto a paper plate; he smiled at his act of servitude. He knew it was a requirement of each eighth-grader at Beaumont Christian to complete at least 100 service hours before graduation. Having finished his treatment session early made Alex consider logging some time helping others.

On Thursday afternoon, two days later, Alex met with several teammates and their parents to serve the homeless inside the lunchroom at Ertter Events. They gathered in the cooking area and distributed hot food to those waiting in line. Each family had to bring a homemade dish, and everyone brought their signature platters.

"Hey Alex," Phil said, setting a chicken cutlet onto an older man's plate and turning. "We've missed you at workouts lately."

"Yeah." Alex tightened the clear plastic glove around his hand. "I've had treatment all week and everything."

"How's that going?" Phil pulled an arm across his chest. "It's probably tiring as heck."

"Yup." Alex scooped another spoonful of spaghetti and laid some on another plate. "The worst part is how sore I am after, though. It's awful."

Alex wasn't going to bring it up. He had made plenty of progress throughout the week but couldn't guess when he'd return. Ruminating over finally making it through the entire session without quitting left Alex encouraged.

There was one more huge hurdle to overcome before starting team workouts with everyone again.

"Doesn't Vance help you out after?" Phil's eyes widened. "And give you ice packs."

"Yes!" Alex lowered his voice. "But it tightens up so much when he does. It's so annoying."

"Darn," Phil patted Alex on the back. "Don't give up. You'll get there."

"I know." Alex nodded. "It's taking forever."

Alex turned his attention to distributing food. He couldn't fret over his treatment sessions all night. Finding that he was most content when he cheered others up or volunteered left Alex glad he was helping.

It's nice to know that you're making a difference.

Shortly after all the people had gotten their food, Alex went straight to the regular high-top table he occupied during lunch. He found Nick, Landon, and Phil already settled in their seats. While plating himself next to his best friend, Alex nearly lost his footing but somehow came to rest.

"Did you guys meet anybody interesting?" Nick said, his arms folded on the table.

"I connected with a veteran," Landon leaned back. "He had PTSD when he came back from Iraq."

"I talked with a few kids who were our age." Alex frowned. "Their mom walked out after their dad lost everything in the 2008 financial crash."

"That's terrible!" Phil's jaw nearly dropped. "It's a good thing we came from great families that love and support us."

Alex contemplated the different stories he had heard. He was grateful for interacting with those outside his bubble of privilege. Even as he recognized how important it was to appreciate what he had instead of what he didn't, it served as a consistent reminder for Alex when things weren't going his way.

Even when you think everything's awful, it could always be worse.

At that moment, Alex's mom shouted from nearby, "Let's go, sweetheart, we've got to meet your dad and brothers for dinner!"

#

Alex felt his heart pounding. He knew his dad wanted an update on his injury. Seeing more of his dad than usual for the next few weeks since the House and Senate were on recess left Alex feeling mixtures of anxiety and dread.

As much as I love dad, I hate getting scolded.

"So, Alex," Mr. Tomassini said, swallowing a piece of filet mignon. "Can you explain why you're behind on your treatment plan?"

Alex's immediate reaction was to roll his eyes. He realized, however, that a small act of disrespect would immediately get called out. Deep down, being called out in front of his family burned Alex like a nasty sting from a yellow jacket. It was both embarrassing and irritating. Since he knew how his dad operated, there was no way he could dodge the question, so he decided honesty couldn't hurt.

"I couldn't finish the session on Tuesday." Alex stared at his dad, who returned the gaze by arrogantly tipping his head. "My legs gave out on my last lap."

The two sat at a small table inside Siemian's Steakhouse a short while later. Mrs. Tomassini planted herself next to her husband and worked on a stuffed chicken breast. Alex settled in between his brothers. Vincent dunked a chicken tender into a cup of ranch dressing.

Although Alex expected his dad to grill him over that answer, he couldn't imagine it being any worse than last week. He'd noticed the verbal beatdowns seemed to get increasingly awful every time. Not sure what more he could do to please his dad made Alex feel worthless.

Will anything I do ever be good enough?

"Which is why you've got to warm up before," Mr. Tomassini drank a Budweiser. "I don't care if you're using a stationary bike or stretching, but you can't brush off loosening up."

"But Dad." Alex pleaded. "I did warm-up, stationary bike and all. I guess I wasn't ready for the next stage yet."

"Obviously not," Mr. Tomassini's voice was condescending. "If you were, you'd be sprinting by now, not spending time getting iced."

"That's unfair, Dad!" Alex's face blushed. "You're not around enough to see how hard I work out."

Alex knew that he'd crossed the line by standing up for himself. He had to let his dad know his voice and opinions matter just as much as everyone else's. As he thought over a snappy comeback, Alex realized things would only get more heated if he continued arguing.

I don't want to be the perfect son.

At that moment, the conversation switched to S.J.'s school prospects to ease tensions that overwhelmed the Tomassini family.

"Hey, S.J.," Mrs. Tomassini said, gulping a glass of white wine. "Did you finalize your school list yet?"

"Almost, mom," S.J. buttered a large roll. "I've got a few more applications to complete."

"For which institutions?" Mr. Tomassini interjected. "I hope you've considered Yale and Georgetown."

Sitting there with his arms crossed, Alex felt out of place. He hadn't had a terrific week as it was and would have instead not joined his family for dinner. Consumed with gut feelings of anxiety and sadness, Alex believed he had nothing of value to offer more than ever after his dad chastised him. As of late, there were times when he wondered what life might be like in another family where he lived as just another average teenager with expectations that weren't always lofty.

"Of course, Dad." S.J. nibbled on a rack of ribs. "I'd prefer public over private universities; a degree is a degree."

"Ivy Leagues hold much more values than state universities, son," Mr. Tomassini said with certainty only he could. "They look not only good on resumes but also open many doors."

It wasn't a well-kept secret that there were different standards between Alex and S.J. He recognized that their dad's controlling ways had limits. Even though he believed that his older brother could major in anything and attend whichever school he wanted and succeed, it made Alex feel inadequate. It was hard for Alex because he felt like he consistently got the short end of the stick.

"I know, Dad." S.J. smiled. "I also sent applications to Chapel Hill, UCLA, Louisville, and UConn Greenbriar as a safety school.

"Wherever you enroll will be lucky to have you," Mrs. Tomassini said. "And we'll support your decision whatever you decide."

Alex hoped his family would be half this enthusiastic when it came time for his eighth-grade graduation in June. He wasn't sure whether he'd attend a private high school or try public, and it was too early to decide. However, all Alex cared about was getting healthy and back on the field, whatever it took. Although rusty at first, Alex knew he would eventually be better than ever once he worked out again.

Chapter Thirteen
Outlasting the Opposition

Alex was winded. They were home against Montclair Academy, and the game couldn't be more lopsided. The Seahawks seemed to have a significant advantage between goals, defensive stops, and tough saves. They seemed intent to score at will with less than two minutes to play before halftime, and the game was unlikely to change anytime soon.

"Not acceptable," Alex imagined his father saying and found himself agreeing. Alex stepped in front of a pass intended for Seahawk midfielder J.P. Magliaro in Beaumont Christian territory and looked for an open teammate who could make a difference. *Enough is enough,* he thought. It's *time to score*. Alex dribbled past Seahawk defenders inside the center circle and nearly sent them on their backs as they tried but failed to claim possession. He spied Phil crossing toward the left corner inside Seahawk territory and flicked the ball his way, optimistic that this drive would put them on the scoreboard.

Phil drew a double-team almost right away, and Alex observed with a raised eyebrow as his teammate faced pressure. Phil deftly dodged a tackle and sent a crossing pass outside the penalty box, where Landon was ready and waiting. Landon's leg went up and over in a bicycle kick as he blasted a shot toward the net.

Please let this be a goal. We need some momentum now.

A collective "great job" rose from the visitor's side of the bleachers as Montclair Academy's goalie snagged the ball then skied it downfield, where white-and-navy blue jerseys awaited its arrival.

"Nice setup, dude," Landon said, matching strides with Alex past the center circle. "That should've been a goal."

"Right." Alex put his hands on his hips. "No worries, though. We'll get the next one."

"We'd better," Landon's voice mixed between frustration and determination. "No way Montclair Academy shuts us out today."

"Quit yapping, boys," Coach Schallhorn called out from the home touchline, shaking his head, "Magliaro's coming up fast."

Alex turned and found J.P. zooming past Phil and Ram's defense en route toward the goal. He raced on an angle to prevent the short, shifty, sandy-blond haired Seahawk midfielder from setting himself for yet another shot. Suddenly feeling familiar sharp pains in his calf, Alex not only found himself tasting grass but holding his lower leg with both hands when he failed.

Alex felt like he couldn't catch a break. He'd returned from the pulled hamstring not long ago, and now his calf was giving him trouble. As he wondered if his sudden cramps resulted from not being in game shape, Alex had a sense of doubt that he'd rushed back.

If I get reinjured, I'll get accused of not stretching enough or logging enough time during workouts.

"You alright?" Kellen squatted beside his teammate just outside their team's penalty box. "That was a nasty wipeout, dude."

"No, Kellen." Alex twisted his face in disgust. "My calf tightened up."

"Let me help you," Kellen said, reaching for his teammate's stiffened leg, "so you can get back on offense."

"No!" Alex shook his head at his teammate's offer. "Just help me up."

Alex launched himself to his feet with Kellen's help but shrieked. He nodded in gratitude and hobbled up field basically on one leg, with each step more challenging than the next. Studying Phil dribbling past the halfway line and approaching Seahawk territory, Alex smiled until defenders instantaneously surrounded his best friend. Feeling his heartbeat double in speed as danger neared Phil, Alex shuffled in his teammate's direction, marked by J.P.

"Hey, Phil," Alex grunted through his teeth as he stumbled around nearby and waved his hand, "I'm open over here, man."

Within seconds, Alex saw his teammate crumble to the ground along with numerous defenders as the ball popped loose. He bit the inside of his lip as he raced after it and instantaneously bumped shoulders with J.P. outside the center circle. Holding back tears in his eyes while claiming possession a mere second before his opponent, Alex turned and flashed ahead. Approaching Seahawk territory with J.P. hot on his heels, Alex recognized it was time to make a move, severe cramp or not.

Alex didn't want to rush this scoring opportunity since the clock was winding down. Instead, he trapped the ball between his legs and heard labored breathing behind opponents. Weaving his way into the middle of the penalty box, Alex distributed a pass toward Landon but winced.

As Alex hopped backward outside Montclair Academy's penalty box to find his teammate taking the pass off his cleat, he put weight on his toes and lifted his heels. He remained on high alert as Seahawk defenders immediately double-teamed Landon. Almost as quickly, he heard shouting and screaming nearby. Alex hurried the best he could to where teammates had gotten pushed, retrieved the ball near the touchlines, and planned his opportunity.

Ten seconds left on the clock. It's showtime. Alex brushed shoulders with several defenders, including J.P. He wanted to be the hero who scored the goal that started Ram's rally before halftime. He wanted that more than anything. So, while feinting right and fake-passing to his best friend on the wing to draw away a defender, Alex dribbled ahead to get a better shot. Once he reached the penalty box and gained separation from his opponents, Alex decided it was time.

With all the strength he could muster, Alex sprinted toward the goal. He took a step back and then launched a shot toward the upper corner of the net. Half expecting the Seahawk goalie who'd stopped everything thrown at him to notch another save, Alex heard Beaumont Christian fans shout and cheer as the ball rippled across the net.

Although they played soccer, not American football, Alex compared the moment and its energy to a two-minute drill in the NFL where the quarterback drove the field's length to get a score before the half or win the game. He wasn't sure what shape his team would be in if he hadn't scored, which made the goal even more important. Even as he imagined what the second half would look like, it forced Alex to consider how much he'd contribute after halftime.

It will be like going to war, only on a soccer field, not the battlefield.

Looking to his left to find Phil staggering toward him, Alex checked his teammate out. He noticed the Ram midfielder flexing his head from side to side, then shrugged. Remembering his best friend's anxiety skyrocketing over getting crushed by their opponents, Alex hoped Phil wasn't hurt. As both boys draped their arms around each other and limped toward the touchlines, the toll this first half had taken on them was evident.

"You, ok?" Alex gasped for every breath.

"I think," Phil said, almost unsure of himself. "I just got the wind knocked out of me."

Moments later, the whistle blew. Score: Away, 4, Rams 1.

It was just a start, but he'd take it. Alex was not only happy that his team was finally on the scoreboard for intermission. He'd receive a well-earned and much-needed breather to rehydrate and work out his cramp. However, one more half remained, and this grueling matchup was far from over.

#

Things only seemed to get worse in the second half. With the score cut in some measure as Beaumont Christian still trailed 5-2, both teams continued giving everything. There was no shortage of physicality either, with punishing slide tackles, accidental contact, and occasional injuries intensifying. Nevertheless, less than twenty minutes remained in regulation, and Montclair Academy controlled.

Alex hauled in a pass from Egan outside Beaumont Christian's penalty box. He turned and raced toward the center mark. Passing through the center circle and immediately surrounded by countless defenders, Alex recognized he'd just gotten rid of the ball.

"Let's go, Alex," Phil streaked past the halfway line but halted when he saw his teammate in trouble. "Pass it here. I'm open, bud."

Alex felt like his chest would implode. Instead, he cut hard past one defender, then another, buying him some breathing room. Then, hearing labored breathing approaching and understanding that meant contact, Alex lofted a pass toward his teammate on the left.

"Hey, Tomassini!" Landon called out from the right touchline. "I got you on the right."

Alex tumbled over and whined, feeling multiple opponents slam into him from all sides. He remembered Coach Schallhorn always reminding them to look out for each other during rivalry games. Then, unable to handle much more high-intensity tackles, Alex sensed the sharp pains in his calf from just before halftime flaring up again. Although this time, Alex feared it was much worse than before.

Something's wrong. I hope I can keep playing.

As strenuous as it was playing Greenbriar Day, Alex considered Montclair Academy ten times worse. He never noticed how most Seahawk players were always fresher than their Rams counterparts, particularly on defense. *It did make sense why Montclair Academy had such a deep bench.* He could never figure out why Coach Schallhorn hardly ever subbed kids out despite having quite a few reserves. Alex also didn't forget how his coach was a huge believer in cross-training or training players to play multiple positions, so lineup adjustments remained simple.

Pushing himself up to a knee, Alex viewed the action. He saw Phil booting the ball along the left touchline and cut right. Now, back on his feet and cheering on his best friend, Alex hoped his teammates could mount a comeback.

"Come on, Phil." Alex dashed toward Seahawk territory the best he could manage. "You've got this man."

At that moment, a Seahawk defender came in for a tackle and collided with Phil, jarring the ball loose. Alex spotted his teammate lying on the field, stretched out as the ball rolled toward the touchline. A throw-in would kill their momentum, so he flashed to the ball ahead of his teammate, who was slow to recover and trapped it between his feet. He eyed the Seahawk defender who tackled Phil, still struggling to get up, then frantically searched for an open teammate. Landon and Nick were both covered. There was no time to stall.

Alex took a deep breath, slashing into Seahawk territory, feinted right, and fired a shot with the inside of his right foot. If he were lucky, it'd be a goal or even sail wide right for a goal kick so he could get a breather. Unfavorably, this result was not the case, as the Seahawk goalkeeper caught the ball with ease. Alex reached down and kneaded his tight calf.

Come on, man, why *can't we score already?*

Alex considered getting subbed out, but the Seahawk goalkeeper rolled a pass out to J.P. and shattered that hope. As he'd done earlier, J.P. dribbled and cut, then weaved his way down the field, threading the ball between one Ram and another. Alex was more frustrated than his teammates for not stopping his opponent but had to admire J.P.'s act of plagiarism.

Impressed or not, Alex couldn't allow Magliaro to score. Instead, Alex darted toward his opponent with everything he had left and caught up with him as J.P. inched closer to Beaumont Christian's penalty box. Going in for a tackle as his opponent drew his leg back for a shot, Alex decided this time would be different.

Alex flicked the ball free. He crashed into his opponent, and both landed hard on the ground. Sniffling as his calf constricted tighter than a wet boot, Alex stared at purple skies transition from light to dark. Wondering how much he had left in the tank, Alex felt like he was running on fumes.

"Yo, Alex." J.P. was on his feet first and offered a hand. "That was a great tackle, dude."

"Uh, thanks." Alex waved off his rival's hand after immediately sensing his pain raging worse than a California wildfire. "You've been on fire all afternoon."

Alex loved playing against J.P. It was challenging to keep up with his opponent's blazing speed and skill on the field. However, Alex believed the Montclair Academy midfielder was probably one of the fastest and best players in the PAC-7.

I can keep up with almost anyone, but I couldn't beat Magliaro in a foot race.

The whistle blew, and Alex gripped his calf with both hands.

"Hang in there, Tomassini," Coach Schallhorn said, jogging onto the field and knelt beside his player. "You'll be okay soon."

Alex heard his coach's encouragement but cried out. He rose his head to see Vance standing over him and pressing the front of his cleats forward. As the pain grew more intense when the Beaumont Christian athletic trainer lifted his leg and continued the movement, Alex covered his eyes. While seizing hold of teammates' hands who pulled him to his feet, Alex laid his arms around their shoulders and then gazed into the stands as his cleats barely swept the grass. As Alex gazed into the stands, he saw Connor sitting with his family.

"You've got this, Alex," teammates bumped fists and patted him on the back as his cleats glided across the grass toward the Rams touchline. "Just drink some water and chill out."

Alex settled onto his team's bench with a wince. He grabbed a cup of water from the team manager and sipped it. Reaching down to knead his tightened calf muscle with his fingers, Alex heard increased shouting on the field and frowned.

I should be out there—stupid cramp.

It was almost déjà vu for Alex, who pondered if he couldn't play anymore. He couldn't help but beat himself up over not drinking enough water or not stretching during intermission. Even as he gazed up at the countless stars lighting up the night skies full of promise, Alex lifted a silent prayer to the heavens to get him back onto the field.

Lord, if it's your will, put me back in the game.

Oliver Hawksworth, a reserve midfielder with messy dark brown hair who'd taken Alex's place, dribbled outside the center circle, and searched for an open teammate back on the field. First, he eyed Landon tiptoeing along the right touchline, then spun around, which caused the Seahawk defender marking him to fall over. Then, Oliver lofted a pass in the Ram right midfielder's direction with the opening his teammate needed.

As Landon collected the ball off his cleat in mid-stride and dashed into the opponent's territory, he faked past one defender before a Seahawk collided with him. He advanced near the penalty box and then found himself surrounded by numerous opponents.

"Yo Land," Nick said, flashing to where his teammate was. "Pass it, buddy. I'm open!"

Seeing this from the Rams bench only made Alex want to be out there more. He set a cold pack on his still constricted calf and sighed. Then, spotting Coach Schallhorn passing by the bench, Alex leaned forward and tapped his coach on the shoulder. Although the chances were slim, Alex figured he'd ask if he could sub back in yet.

"No way, Alex," Coach Schallhorn responded. "It's only been two minutes, and you've still got to use heat and stretch."

"Darn it," Alex muttered to himself, or at least he thought. "Coach doesn't trust me anymore."

"Yes, he does," a reserve Ryan scooted next to him. He wore a royal blue warmup suit. "You just need to loosen your calf."

At that moment, from somewhere in the home stands, Connor yelled, "Let's go, Rams!"

Alex was about to turn around when something on the field caught his attention first. There was a pile of players from both teams on the ground. He counted less than a minute before the ball emerged and rolled away. Leaning forward now, Alex watched with great interest as boys from Beaumont Christian, and Montclair Academy pounced on it like a Tiger chasing its prey.

The Rams were still trailing by three with just under twelve minutes to play in regulation. He scanned Montclair Academy's side of the field and spotted several teammates, including Landon, who'd finally recovered and started breaking away from defenders. Bumping shoulders with J.P. and dribbling into Seahawk territory as cleats struck his legs, Oliver studied his teammate's slow movements and raised an eyebrow.

"Hey, Oli," Phil raced around nearby with a defender hot on his heels. "Pass it over here quick."

Oliver feinted left then right past another would-be defender. He booted the pass in mid-stride to Phil before stumbling to the ground. Landing hard on his back, Oliver immediately sprung to his feet. Adrenaline kicked in.

If nothing else, Alex had to admit he was impressed. He hadn't seen Oliver tested by more formidable opponents, as everyone they faced during his brief absence were softer losing teams, which made this display sweeter. If his teammates could score at least one goal and make a big defensive stop, Alex believed they had a chance.

Helped onto the grass beside their team's bench, Alex wrapped his hands around his head. He raised the stiffened leg in the air and looked up at Vance. As the Beaumont Christian athletic trainer held his heel and thrust the front of Alex's cleats forward, he shrieked. Hoping the cramps subsided soon, Alex covered his eyes and tried hiding the pain.

Reminded of what seemed like the longest two weeks of treatment in his life, Alex had no intention of landing back in the trainer's room indefinitely. He'd tired of following the treatment plan almost every day, doing exercises, icing, and stretching. Not wanting the only preparation or post-game itinerary to include spending time with Vance forced Alex to consider how often he put himself on the line for his team.

Phil instantly feinted past a defender and then dashed into Montclair Academy's penalty box. He pulled the ball into open space and then lifted his leg. Firing a shot toward the goal, Phil sensed an opponent right before he crashed into him.

The ball floated toward the net and turned right. Montclair Academy's goalie flashed toward it and dove. His face tasted grass as the ball bounced just past him.

Back to his feet now, Alex saw his teammates celebrating and heard subsequent cheers from Beaumont Christian fans. He turned and high-fived Ryan, whose bright blue eyes matched his uniform. Reaching over to check his calf, Alex found the awful tightness subside, but tolerable soreness remained.

I can play through discomfort, he thought, *but am I ready?*

"Start warming up, Alex," Coach Schallhorn said, glancing at the Rams captain. "You're going back in."

Alex nodded, and his heart leaped. He jogged up and down the touchlines while mixing in dynamic movements. Gazing at the scoreboard, Alex realized the Rams were down by two with 8:30 left. Alex slapped Oliver a high-five, trotting over to join his team's starters huddled around Coach Schallhorn.

"Great job, man." Alex smiled. "That was a heck of an effort."

"Uh, thanks." Oliver shrugged. "I tried, but it's hard to fill your spot in the lineup. Nobody plays like you, though."

"Not true." Alex shook his head. "You've got to play the best you're capable of; that's all anyone can ask."

As Alex slipped into a circle of teammates gathered around their coach, his chest swelled with hope. He was returning after dealing with severe cramps. Half listening to the game plan, Alex looked around at his comrades, particularly Phil, whose hands were on his hips and drenched in sweat.

Everybody must dig deep, he thought. We can still tie this game up.

"Rams on 3: 1-2-3!" Coach Schallhorn hollered as the boys placed their hands atop his.

"Rams!" the ten starters shouted as they broke the huddle.

The whistle blew, and players from both teams hustled onto the field.

Just when Alex set up at his attacking mid position, he felt a nudge on his shoulder. He turned and saw Phil smiling. Checking his best friend out, Alex noticed that Phil's posture and body language suggested someone who'd worked all game tirelessly long.

"Glad your back on the field," Phil said, lifting his leg toward his chest. "You came back just in time."

"Right." Alex stood on his feet and lifted his heels. "You guys played very well without me, though."

"True," Phil ran a hand through his sweaty hair. "But we all play off your enthusiasm and passion, and we count on you for leadership."

Almost instantly, the whistle blew as play resumed.

For the next six and half minutes or so, Montclair Academy's intentions were trying to waste time and run down the clock, and Alex knew it. He and his Ram teammates waited patiently to capitalize on any opponent mistakes. Hearing Coach Schallhorn shouting to be more aggressive on defense, Alex and other Ram midfielders stayed on the Seahawk offense like birds on a feeder. While matching J.P.'s every move in the blink of an eye, Alex intercepted a pass meant for his rival from a

Seahawk center back outside the penalty box, then fired a shot into the right corner of the net. Goal!

The Rams only trailed by one now as the scoreboard read: Away 5, Rams, 4.

Alex collected a pass from Egan outside Beaumont Christian's penalty box with around two minutes to play. J.P., on the instant, marked him as he dribbled past the center mark. Feeling his opponent's cleats striking his lower legs and grunting, Alex searched for a passing channel he could squeeze the ball into even if it were tight. Spying a small nugget of space between Phil and his defender close by, Alex sent a pass in his best friend's direction.

Falling face-first onto the grass, Alex lifted his head to view the action. He saw the Ram midfielder advance the ball into Seahawk territory, then loft a cross pass to the right. As he peeked to the right and spotted J.P. wriggling in pain, Alex frowned. Once he pushed himself up, Alex trotted over to his fallen opponent and checked on him.

"Hey!" Alex said, noticing his rival pulling his knees toward his chest. "You ok, man?"

"Oh, hey, Alex." J.P. sniffled. "Yeah, my back started spasming. Can you give me a hand?"

"Yeah, sure." Alex pressed J.P.'s knees further. "I hate when that happens."

Just as quickly, Alex heard shouting up the field and flashed ahead. He halted outside Montclair Academy's penalty box and noticed Landon double-teamed and under duress. Sprinting around and waving for a pass, Alex tried to attract his teammate's attention. Then, cringing as the Ram player went down hard and the ball bounced off, Alex chased after it, followed by two Seahawk defenders.

Trapping it between his feet near the halfway line, Alex gazed at the scoreboard. He saw less than a minute remained and knew it was time. Outrunning the Seahawk players from before, Alex raced into the opponent's territory. Feinting past one white-and-royal blue jersey and sprinting past another, Alex faked-passed left to Phil, then approached the penalty box. Pushing the ball back slightly right with the outside of his foot and lifting his leg, Alex fired a shot.

The ball glided toward Montclair Academy's goalie and veered right. The Seahawk defender keeper flashed toward it, then dove. This time around, though, he tipped it with his fingertips before it rolled straight out of play.

The whistle blew, and Alex put his hands on his knees.

"Oh, come on already." Alex splattered out clear mucus on the ground.

"Corner kick, blue!" the referee pointed to a flag in the right corner of Montclair Academy's side of the field.

Alex dashed to the right corner, where a referee set the ball. He backpedaled three steps, then studied some teammates lining up behind each other at the penalty spot. Not knowing how far or effectively he could boot the ball with the calf soreness, Alex eyed Nick and Xavier inside Montclair Academy's goalie box on either side, then thought, *We've got to score, whatever it takes*.

The whistle blew as play resumed.

Alex took a deep breath and sprinted to the ball. He surveyed teammates flashing off in various directions before spotting Nick inching outside the goalie box. Lifting his leg and instantly feeling an aching sensation in his calf, Alex fired the ball toward Montclair Academy's penalty box. Dashing ahead with everything he had to follow his kick, Alex trusted his teammates would do their part.

Phil raced just outside Montclair Academy's penalty box, then eyed the ball. Instead, he leaped in the air and collided with an opponent. Heading a pass to the right before falling, Phil landed hard on his side next to his opponent.

A Seahawk center nearby immediately blocked the ball and sent a pass in the direction of a teammate at the center circle.

Stepping in front of another pass intended for J.P., Alex flashed toward Seahawk territory as his opponent trailed behind. He felt J.P. slamming into him and bumped shoulders. While approaching the Montclair Academy penalty box and eying a teammate, making a beeline toward the goal, Alex understood he must seize the opportunity. Alex booted a pass toward Landon and then sent a silent prayer for a goal.

Landon sprinted to where the ball was and gathered it in mid-stride. He faked out a defender and then knocked a shot toward the goal before an opponent slammed him. Landing hard on the ground, Landon writhed in pain and pounded the ground.

The ball flew toward Montclair Academy's net and veered left. The Seahawk goalkeeper surged in its direction but stumbled inches away before the ball's arrival. As Alex dashed toward the goal box in case of a rebound, his heart leaped. After giving everything on the field, making all the right passes, or hoping he did, Alex wondered if this was the lucky break the Rams waited for all game long. Then, watching the ball ripple against the left corner of the net, Alex raised his arms in triumph.

The Rams, at long last, tied the score at 5 with no time left in regulation.

At the final whistle, Alex headed to the Ram touchlines beside Phil. He and his best friend draped arms around each other's shoulders for support. Dropping onto the bench like a zombie army due to exhaustion and pain, Alex grabbed a cup of water from the student manager. Then, feeling a slap on his thigh from his teammate, Alex turned to Phil and widened his eyes.

"That last play was epic," Phil smiled. "The way you set up that corner kick and everything, I knew we'd score and tie it up."

"Thanks, man." Alex reached over and kneaded his calf. "Gosh darn it, my leg tightened up, and we've got overtime soon."

"Not good!" Phil said. "Should I get Vance?"

"No way." Alex stood up but felt an unimaginable pain in his lower leg and sat back down. "Can you give me a hand?"

"Yup," Phil slapped his teammate on the back. "As long as you help me out, my quads are burning."

Settling beside the bench and raising his leg in the air, Alex whined when his best friend pushed the front of his cleats. Despite how much stretching hurt, he couldn't bear the thought of being on the touchlines again during overtime. Looking up in the home stands and seeing Connor still sitting with his family, Alex pointed in that direction.

"Sure." Alex twisted his face in agony as his calf throbbed. "Hey, check out Connor up there."

"I saw him earlier," Phil pushed on his best friend's cleats once more before stretching out his hand. "What's he doing with your parents?"

Alex shrugged. He didn't know what his former close friend was doing up there any more than he knew the outcome during overtime. Wondering how well he'd hold up during overtime, Alex took hold of Phil's hand and was helped up. Then, helping his best friend stretch his stiff quads, Alex recognized there was nothing he could do except wait and see how things played out.

Chapter Fourteen
Needing the Narrative

"So, mom", Alex said, sliding his iPhone into the pocket of his khaki pants, "how did you end up agreeing to counsel Connor again?"

"I already told you, sweetheart," Mrs. Tomassini sipped her Pumpkin Spice Late and let it back into the cupholder. "He came to watch the game on Saturday night and saw us sitting. When I waved him over to say hello, Connor told me he needed to talk."

"Oooh, ok." Alex's face brightened with intrigue. "Did you tell you where he's been?"

"You know I can't tell you that," Mrs. Tomassini shot her son a look of disappointment. "I can say that Connor plans to talk with you at school today about everything."

Early Monday morning, Mrs. Tomassini drove Alex and Vincent to school in her dark-colored SUV. His mom was in the driver's seat, Alex rested in the front passenger's seat, and Vincent sat behind his older brother. They approached the entrance to Beaumont Christian School, but Alex still had so many questions swirling around his mind.

Alex felt his stomach tighten. He hadn't talked with his former buddy in almost a month. Having not seen Connor much, if at all, except occasionally on campus left Alex wondering if the kid was ok—not just saying it but meaning it.

The last I saw Connor during workouts, he went off.

"Here we are, boys," Mrs. Tomassini rolled her car to a stop in front of Sullivan Science and Technology Center between her son's buildings. "Make today a great one."

"Thanks, mom," the boys said, in sync with each other while opening their doors and climbing out with backpacks.

As Alex made the short walk to Humphrey Hall, he remained puzzled about Connor. He couldn't start to imagine everything his former buddy had been through. Although he realized his mom took privacy laws against disclosing information very seriously, it only made Alex even more curious about Connor's struggles.

Why would Connor reach out to mom and not me?

"Great game, Saturday! You guys rocked! The last shot stunned the Seahawks!"

Hearing cheers from classmates inside the crowded hallways of Humphrey Hall now, Alex headed toward his locker. First, he exchanged high-fives and fist bumps with peers congratulating him on Saturday's Ram victory. Alex felt an arm on his shoulder while putting up his backpack in the designated locker and organizing binders for the first few classes. As he turned and saw Connor standing over his shoulder with a half-smile, Alex's heartbeat doubled in speed.

Back on his feet, now leaning against lockers, Alex noticed something different about his former close friend. He knew it wasn't the clothes because his classmate always dressed to impress, strikingly on chapel days. Giving him a once-over, Alex realized that Connor's face was much brighter than he remembered, and his former teammate gave the impression of being happier.

Hopefully, Connor's doing better than before. He was a mess last time.

"Hey," Connor said, stuffing his hands into his pockets. "Do you want to walk to chapel together?"

"Sure, man." Alex nodded. "How are things? My mom said you had wanted to talk about what's been going on."

"That's right," Connor turned to Alex. "I'm doing ok, much better than I had been."

"What's been going on?" Alex raised an eyebrow. "Nobody's seen you since you went off during workouts?"

While trotting together toward Cardinale Chapel, Alex listened to his classmate's version of events.

"That's when everything went downhill," Connor hung his head. "My dad and I got into an argument over my 'tantrum' his words which evolved into a screaming match."

"Oh snap." Alex twisted his face in surprise. "That's terrible."

"And then he sent me to my room," Connor explained. "But I threw some clothes in my duffel bag and snuck out my window."

"No way!" Alex's eyes bulged. "Where did you go?"

Hearing the beginnings of Connor's story was enough for Alex to feel at least an ounce of compassion for his classmate. He recalled when he and his close friends hung out with Connor at his house and learned of the family troubles. Having no idea what transpired after the outburst at team workouts left Alex feeling guilty for not being a better friend.

If I'd been there for Connor, maybe he wouldn't have melted down.

"Clontz's café to call Egan," Connor admitted. "His family let me stay overnight before my mom picked me up in the morning."

"Did she listen at least?" Alex turned and studied his classmate. "Or did she let you down like everyone else?"

"My mom listened to what happened," Connor's heart sank. "But it didn't matter since the school called my house about how I've acted out recently."

"Oh, man." Alex patted his classmate on the back. "What did they say?"

Alex feared the worst about his classmate. He wasn't sure what could've happened except getting sick or enduring corporal punishment. Even though he and Connor weren't friends at present, it still bothered Alex that someone he'd grown up with was hurting, and he couldn't do anything to help.

"That I needed to see someone before I could return to school," Connor cleared his throat. "So, my parents took me to a mental health facility to get evaluated; it was awful."

"Shut the front door!" Alex felt the air almost deflate from his lungs. "Is that why you've been absent from school and talked to my mom at our game?"

"Yes!" Connor nodded. "I was diagnosed with an adjustment disorder and depression. It started after my parents split, then only worsened recently."

"I'm sorry, man." Alex sighed. "We're here for you, whatever you need."

Alex was shocked by what Connor had been through. He had no idea how bad things got with him. Wanting to trust that his classmate was getting the help he needed or at the very least was no longer in a dark place left Alex unsure what to think. There was nothing Alex would've liked more than to give his former friend another chance to revive their friendship.

Was Connor ready?

Stepping into Cardinale's chapel entrance, Alex shoved all the thoughts about his classmate into the back of his mind. He tried going into every chapel service with a clear head to hear the readings and homily. Then, seeing Connor kneel and do the sign of the cross before sliding into a chair next to Egan, Alex shook his head.

Maybe he's not ready to sit together yet. Connor will come around eventually.

# #

Sitting at a small table with three other classmates during ninth-period Language Arts for small group discussions, Alex studied a handout provided by Ms. Farnsworth to all members with questions. He considered his friendship with Phil and compared it to their novel. Alex knew his best friend wouldn't ever get himself or them involved in risky behaviors as close as they were. Reading between the lines, Alex found that both characters had a relationship that was anything but simple. It was complicated.

"Let's start with our questions." Alex set the handout on his desk. "Who wants to go first?"

"The narrator returns to the Devon school," Phil spoke first. "He's there fifteen years after the events of the story."

"That's right," Egan interjected. "Gene wants to visit a marble staircase and an old tree."

"Why are they significant?" Alex leaned forward. "They're places that Gene associates with fear."

Alex enjoyed small group discussions with classmates. He thought they were fun and meaningful if everyone participated. It only helped that everyone in Alex's group was a teammate or at least an athlete at school.

"It took place during World War 2." Gavin piped up. "So, the fear from that plus his environmental danger."

"As in Finny, dude," Phil titled his head. "The narrator's roommate doesn't have his best interest at heart."

Alex counted himself lucky in the friendship department. He had a handful of close friends but, more importantly, peers who looked out for him. Although they joked around a lot and ragged on each other, Alex recognized the tight-knit bond with most classmates.

That's how things are at Beaumont Christian School. We're family.

"That leads into chapter two." Alex ran his finger down the list. "With Finny not having Gene's best interests in mind, what happens between them in this section? How do these things make the narrator feel?"

"Mr. Prudhomme intends on disciplining Finny and Gene for missing dinner," Egan smiled. "But the substitute teacher is swayed by Finny's charisma and lets them both off."

"Right." Alex nodded. "But why is there tension between the two?"

"Gene thinks Finny can get away with anything," Gavin said. "Including wearing a pink shirt that the narrator thinks makes his roommate look homophobic."

Alex contrasted his family dynamic with S.J. to the characters in their novel. He wasn't envious of his older brother's talent or ability to get out of trouble. Alex's view of things was more about getting recognized for his accomplishments than competing. Alex didn't want or need others to believe he was a superstar. His play on the field spoke for itself. He was mainly concerned with proving it to himself.

"It takes a strong kid to wear pink, dude," Phil pointed out. "You've got to be comfortable with yourself as a boy."

Hearing the clicking of shoes against tiled floors nearby, Alex expected Ms. Farnsworth any minute now. He didn't know if their teacher overheard any part of their conversation. It wasn't as if anything they said was off-topic, which usually got a student in trouble. Although they hadn't progressed through many questions, Alex understood that everyone had a lot to say.

"Very well, Mr. Larson," Ms. Farnsworth looked over four students seated at the front of her classroom. "At Beaumont Christian, we embrace all our brothers and sisters, specifically those in the LGBTQ community. Tolerance is one of our core principles."

Alex didn't agree with Ms. Farnsworth often, but on this, he did. He viewed all his peers as brothers and sisters, whether he got along. Lost in thought about the talk with his former close friend, Alex knew they needed to act more understanding.

Suppose Connor was hurting that much, and we didn't hear him out?

Chapter Fifteen
Validating the View

"So, Al," Nick said, taking a bite of his bacon-grilled cheese. "Con's been in the hospital the last few weeks?"

"Yeah, Nick." Alex sipped a Lipton Green Tea. "After everything happened at workouts, he had a huge fight with his parents. So, they checked him in that weekend."

It was two days later Wednesday afternoon, when Alex, Nick, and Phil sat at their usual high-top table in the lunchroom. Since Monday morning, the three friends have discussed what everyone in Humphrey Hall wondered. Where was Connor, and was he ok?

"All because of the divorce?" Nick washed down his lunch with chocolate milk. "I know that Connor had a rough time with it and then lost his position on top of it all. No wonder he flipped."

"What about his spot in the lineup?" Philip spoke up. "You know Coach Schallhorn doesn't care what the reason is for slacking off."

"Agreed, Phil." Alex nodded. "Schallhorn's all about the 'next kid up' mindset."

Alex considered his first season under Coach Schallhorn. He accepted the reserve role and knew he wouldn't see much playing time. Alex desired to learn from the veterans and older kids on the team. It wasn't until the Rams' top midfielder suffered a knee injury that

Alex got his chance, earned all the respect he got, and all the minutes logged.

"I know, I know, Al." Nick lowered his voice. "I think Con got a raw deal, and nobody listened to him."

"Snodgrass got a raw deal?" Phil scoffed. "He walked out on us a day or two before the Greenbriar Day game, then insulted Alex."

"Con was just upset at the moment, Phil." Nick swallowed his grilled cheese. "He didn't mean anything by it."

Alex wouldn't take sides. He understood what both were saying. But, although inclined to agree with his best friend, Alex couldn't show any impartiality.

Why couldn't anyone in school just let everything be?

"The heck he didn't, dude," Phil said, twisting his face in disgust. "Snodgrass has a terrible attitude. I wish he'd transferred."

"You don't mean that, man." Alex turned to his best friend. "You, me, Nick, and Connor have been close friends forever. We've always stood by you whenever you went through hard times."

"True, Al." Nick frowned. "So, why can't you support Con when he needs you most, Phil?"

"No, I meant everything I said, guys," Phil leaned back and crossed his arms. "Connor's such a hotshot who everybody, including my parents, adores, and I'm over it."

Alex's jaw dropped. He heard most of Phil's secrets, insecurities, and dreams throughout their childhood friendship. Not recalling his best friend's jealousy of their teammate made Alex wonder if something else was up. Feeling forced to choose between one or two comrades, Alex sensed his heartbeat double in speed.

There were a few minutes of silence before a group of kids at another table motioned Nick over, and Alex breathed a sigh of relief.

"What was that all about, Phil?" Alex rested a hand on Phil's shoulder. "Is everything ok?"

"Not exactly," Phil sighed. "We'll talk about it later. "Can you come to yoga with me tonight?"

"Sure, man." Alex studied his classmate, then frowned. "Whatever you need."

# #

Alex had never considered yoga a hobby. He had first tried it two summers ago after two-a-day team workouts when Phil invited him. Unsure of what to expect during his first session, Alex found his best friend just as encouraging and passionate in the yoga studio as he had been on the soccer field. Midway through this new experience, Alex had felt more relief from the activity than countless chiropractor visits or anywhere his dad brought him. Alex had to admit any soreness from morning and afternoon workouts had disappeared, and he had accepted Phil's invites ever since.

In a pushup position inside Youkilis Yoga Studio, Alex set his wrists under his shoulders later that day. He hadn't talked to Phil about earlier events in the lunchroom yet. But, knowing he would eventually have to break the ice one way or another, Alex felt more uncertain than ever. Alex even wondered if his best friend wanted another excuse to hang out on a school night.

"Hey, Phil." Alex lowered himself halfway down and kept his arms close. "Did you need to talk about something?"

"Yeah, dude," Phil said, mimicking Alex's movements. "It's just like ever since Connor started having trouble. That's all anyone cares or talks about. As if nobody else's problems mattered or whatever."

"I get that." Alex lifted his feet off the mat. "Things sure seemed that way, especially with soccer stuff and everything going on at school."

"Right." Phil turned to his best friend. "Which is why it's frustrating when nobody noticed how down I was."

Shifting his weight to his right hand and foot, Alex wasn't sure why Phil claimed he was so down. He didn't recall Phil any different than usual except worrying about getting hammered by massive defenders in their last game. That was normal. Aside from casual whining about training session soreness and teachers giving him a hard time, Alex never heard anything he considered problematic from his classmate. But then again, Alex didn't think it wasn't something they'd ever discussed.

"You could've fooled me, man," Alex said. "You're always so upbeat and excited during sports."

"Maybe around you guys," Phil raised his leg and cringed. "But when I'm alone or at home, everything's different."

"How so?" Alex settled onto his back. "I thought you didn't get much downtime since you and your parents are always on the go?"

As Mr. Youkilis moved the class through their final two poses before cooling down, Alex gazed at Phil, who shot him an annoyed look.

"Exactly, dude," Phil said. "We're always moving onto something else, so we never get to talk about anything. And when if I do bring up something that's bothering me, they dismiss it."

"Really?" Alex raised his eyebrows. "Your parents seem super supportive and encouraging."

"That's for show, Alex," Phil admitted. "They continually monitor everything I do, eat, drink, and watch. So, my dad tells me that body image is something only girls struggle with, and I needed to deal with it."

"Harsh." Alex curled his lip. "What did your mom say?"

"That it's normal," Phil's voice cracked. "And to not worry."

Looking around at the nineteen other classmates, most of whom were also adolescents, Alex wondered how many struggled with things no one talked about. He recognized he wasn't only there to support his best friend and alleviate some stress and pain. Not wanting to let Phil down, Alex considered what might lift his classmates' spirits. The best thing Alex sensed he could do was support and be there for his childhood friend in a way he couldn't for their former teammate.

"She's right," Alex said. "Don't stress about getting bigger, man. It's not that serious now."

"I'm tired of being so skinny," Phil shot back. "And getting teased because I'm small and weak."

They continued their conversation as the two lay on their backs for some cooldown stretches.

"What do you mean?" Alex raised his legs toward the ceiling. "You never mentioned anyone teasing you before."

"It's like Kellen and those guys," Phil followed his best friend's movements and kept his legs straight while lowering them. "They're always picking on me because I'm short and have no muscles."

"Don't let it get to you, bud." Alex rested his arms on the floor but groaned. "Kellen can be a jerk sometimes."

"That's an understatement," Phil studied Alex. "I try not to let it bother me, but sometimes those thoughts pop in mind at the worse times."

Alex could relate. There were times, especially this season, when he doubted and cursed his size and what limitations came with it. Comforted by the skills he did possess, like speed, agility, toughness, and others that made him an excellent player, it often left Alex unfazed by things he couldn't do or wasn't in control of.

Chapter Sixteen
Allegiances Analyzed

It was hard for Alex to imagine living through a global pandemic where everyone had to wear masks and social distance. Still, those were precisely the recommendations asked of characters in the movie Contagion. He'd wanted to see the film for over a month now, but his injury and treatment sessions delayed it. Alex sat in the top row of auditorium ten inside Cronenworth Cinemas next to his older brother with his eyes glued to the screen.

It's incredible yet frightening at the same time.

Alex liked to picture himself in whatever movie he watched, and Contagion was no exception. He saw himself as the United States president who led America through the pandemic safely but without overstepping civil liberties or a scientist developing a safe vaccine that would reduce hospitalizations if nothing else. Even while weighing which role, he'd be more likely to fill, Alex settled on the president.

Health emergency or not, the constitution guarantees us certain rights.

Alex and his older brother rehashed their favorite moments from the movie on the ride home in S.J.'s Ridgeline.

"Dr. Cheever and the CDC did their best," S.J. said, turning to Alex and grinning. "Public health isn't the easiest job, especially when you can't please everybody."

"True." Alex pulled an arm across his chest. "But if your messaging isn't consistent, you'll lose trust."

"Agreed," S.J. drummed his fingers against the steering wheel. "But would you have counted on Krumwiede's opinion?"

"The conspiracy theorist?" Alex shielded his eyes from the glare of a streetlight they'd passed. "No way, man, they're the same people who call JFK and 9-11 'inside jobs."

Alex certainly held political beliefs more so than the average thirteen-year-old. He considered his opinions along the lines of common sense and fiscally responsible. At the same time, having a father who was a United States senator was challenging. Alex admitted it wasn't all bad. It certainly had its perks.

I'm the brightest student in Social Studies, so there's that.

"Couldn't have said that any better," S.J. laughed. "What scenes stuck out to you?"

"There were so many." Alex's voice was full of excitement. "That flashback where the rainforest got cleared, and bats dispersed resulting in a pandemic from somebody not washing their hands."

"Pretty crazy, right?" S.J. shook his head. "A chef of all people forgets basic hygiene."

"Right, yeah." Alex cracked his knuckles. "It started with the rainforest clearing by that Beth character's company, sort of situational irony."

If Alex learned nothing else during classes with Farnsworth, he could apply a class term to a movie. He was a massive advocate for environmentalism and taking care of the planet. Even though he wouldn't go as far as to say eliminating fossil fuels was the answer, it was unrealistic. Alex always tried picking up trash whenever he spotted it.

We only have one earth. It's everyone's job to take care of it.

As S.J. turned onto their street and neared the Tomassini home, the conversation gave way to addressing the elephant in the room.

"Hey Alex,' S.J. nudged his little brother on the shoulder. "Are you thinking about giving Connor another chance?"

"I don't know." Alex shrugged. "I want to."

"What's holding you back?" S.J. said, gazing at Alex. "He's a great kid buddy and needs some support."

"I think I'm afraid of Connor letting me down," Alex's voice cracked, "as much as he is someone disappointing him."

If Alex were honest about friendships, Connor would always be a close friend deep down. Not knowing if they'd be the kind of friends they'd been before made Alex unsure of how everything might play out.

I hope we do work things out. Connor and I used to be so tight.

"Absolutely, brother!" S.J. pulled his truck into the family's driveway. "You'll never know unless you try."

"Indeed." Alex reached for the door handle but paused. "I'll wait for a few more sessions and give it a shot."

"Fair enough," S.J. extended a closed fist. "Everything good for now?"

"For now!" Alex bumped his older brother's fist. "Yes!"

Alex climbed out of the truck and strolled toward the front door. He heard chatter and laughter. Figuring mom and Vincent were probably watching a funny TV show or movie, Alex opened the door and stepped inside. His heart leaped when he saw Connor stretched out on the couch with his family.

I didn't see that coming.

"Hey, mom!" Alex called out as he trotted to the living room. "We're home!"

# #

Strolling toward Finley's Fieldhouse with Phil on Friday afternoon, Alex welcomed the moderate breeze on his bare skin from tall trees nearby. He and his best friend had just finished eighth-period language arts and mulled over their weekend plans. Appreciating that not only was school done until next week, but the Rams had a soft game coming up eased Alex's mind, even if temporarily. Hearing chatter and laughter around him, Alex saw teammates passing them by, then smiled.

"So, Alex," Phil's said, his voice full of excitement. "My dad's taking us camping on Bear Mountain after our game tomorrow for a guy's weekend. It'll be a blast."

"Can't, man." Alex frowned. "I've already promised Connor I'd see *Real Steel* with him for his birthday."

"The movies?" Phil looked away. "But that's our thing, dude."

"One of our things." Alex reminded his classmate. "And what's the big deal?"

Alex rubbed his temples. He'd wondered what Phil was thinking, notably after their yoga session, then yesterday's weight training. Although hanging out every weekend was almost guaranteed, Alex felt like he sometimes needed a break. There was something about spending time with different kids at times that he found refreshing.

"I was planning on toasting marshmallows and setting up tents for us," Phil whined. "Plus, my mom already cleared everything with yours."

"Oh yeah?" Alex hung his head in regret. "My mom's been so busy between work and counseling Connor, and I guess she didn't get a chance to tell me."

Alex's heart sank. He wasn't sure what to do. Tormented between choosing between his best friend and repairing a broken friendship only made Alex feel worse. It was one of those times when he wished S.J. was there.

"I guess not, Alex." Phil made a sour face. "Should I just tell my dad you aren't coming?"

"No, Phil," Alex answered. "I can tell Connor something came up, and it's not like he only invited me. He asked me to tag along with him and Egan."

"Third-wheeling it, huh?" Phil smirked. "It shows what he thinks of you, dude. You know I'd never treat you like that."

"I don't know, Phil." Alex ignored Phil's snarky comeback. "Connor's doing so well now. I don't want him to have a—."

"Setback, right?" Phil interrupted. "Stop worrying, bud. It's not your problem!"

Alex realized Phil was right. Regrettably, he'd gotten so caught up with his former close friend's reemergence that he neglected everyone else. The truth was Alex cared too much whether kids felt the same way. It was one of those things that everyone around campus loved about him.

As the fieldhouse side entrance came into view, Alex's heart pounded. He couldn't bring this conversation into the locker room and had to figure out a way to end it. Unsure of how to respond, he could only say a silent prayer.

Why are friendships so hard?

"Yeah, Phil." Alex stepped through the door behind his teammate. "I'll go camping with you and your dad."

"I hope you mean that," Phil said. "I'm pumped about spending the night up there."

Entering the locker room together, Alex could only nod in agreement. He headed to his locker, which was beside Phil's. Alex switched from the school uniform into workout clothes and studied his best friend's demeanor. The last thing he and his teammates needed was another distraction on the field.

Chapter Seventeen
Campout Connections

Understanding that friendships in middle school were complex and challenging was a hard reality that Alex never gave much thought to. He was always surrounded by peers with whom he conversed over school, sports, and the challenges they faced. Although they were close buddies who discussed almost everything in their lives and could work through any disagreement. Alex found himself unsure of how to handle this dispute with Phil.

Sitting in the backseat of Phil's dad, Fletcher's, grey Avalanche, next to his best friend late Saturday afternoon, Alex could only stare out the window. He'd noticed the change of attitude in his teammate for the last few days worsen. Finding Phil's anxiety and moodiness almost impossible to deal with left Alex wishing he'd gotten out of the trip.

What does Phil want?

"So, Alex," Phil's dad said, drinking a medium-sized coffee with cream and sugar. "When was the last time you went to Bear Mountain?"

"I don't remember." Alex crossed one leg over the other and turned the opposite way. "It's been a long time."

"Phil and I camp there at least twice a month," Phil's dad gazed at his son in the rearview mirror. "Isn't that right, son?"

"Yes, Dad," Phil kneaded his quad with his knuckles. "It's our favorite thing to do together."

Fletcher Larson was over six feet and well-built. He had faded light brown hair and friendly blue eyes. As a captain for Greenbriar Police Department, Phil's dad was the type of guy who ran his home the same he conducted himself at work. Although he was Seemingly unable to stop evaluating his son's performance or making sure he was doing what he was supposed to, Fletcher tended to make life difficult for his son and their relationship.

Behind Phil's miserable response was a sad and frustrated teenager who felt forced to camp out with a dad he resented and a best friend he sensed drifting away from. Alex guessed this was going on from hearing his buddy and studying his movements. They hadn't held an entire conversation since entering the locker room on Friday afternoon, and nothing had changed. They had more tension than drivers stuck in bumper-to-bumper traffic on the L.A. freeway during rush hour.

"We're so stoked you were able to join us," Phil's dad changed lanes and zoomed past an eighteen-wheeler. "I told Phil it wouldn't be a guys' weekend without having your best bud around."

"Yes, sir." Alex swallowed a lump in his throat. "I wouldn't have missed it for anything."

"You're such a li—."

"I know you wouldn't have," Phil's dad intervened and shot Phil an eye glare in the mirror. "Phil's very lucky to have such a loyal and kind friend like you, and I remind him all the time."

There was a moment when Phil's dad finished talking, and Phil let out a loud scoff before turning away, leaving Alex more stunned than a boxer jabbed by an unexpected hook. The amount of jealousy and anger that Alex sensed coming from his buddy suggested something more at play than a simple misunderstanding, a lot more. His initial guess was something between his buddy and dad, but it was more profound than that. It suddenly hit Alex like a lightning strike during a thunderstorm. Phil was still infuriated about him considering ditching the campout for a movie with Connor and Egan.

"Yes, Sir!" Alex smiled. "I'm lucky to have him in my life, especially during the sports seasons."

"Agreed," Phil's dad nodded. "You two are like Batman and Robin."

"Nah." Alex shook his head. "We're more like Captain America and Winter Soldier."

"That's it!" Phil's dad extended his large hand backward for a high-five, and both boys slapped him. "Being best buds means they know what each does before it happens."

The comparison wasn't wrong either, in Alex's opinion. He'd known Phil forever, and they were in sync most times. Even accepting there was nothing he could do to change things now frustrated Alex.

If nothing else, at least hiking up to Bear Mountain and setting up tents with Phil reassured Alex that his best bud didn't hate him. It forced them to work together and lean on each other to do the climb. Understanding how much of a biblical connection between him and Phil's tiff left Alex feeling confident sooner than later. They'd work everything out.

For the present, though, they couldn't have been further apart.

# #

"I think you're overreacting."

Alex raised the main tent poles on one side. He'd been helping his best friend set their tent in the campgrounds of Bear Mountain since making their journey up. Although they'd looked out for each other around many sharp curves and made sure either found themselves in danger, Alex wasn't convinced it was for the betterment of friendship.

Even though we're fighting, neither of us wants the other hurt.

"Am I?" Phil worked on his side but shot his friend a sour look. "All you've seemed to care about lately is Connor and making sure he's ok."

"Yeah, well." Alex avoided eye contact. "Look at everything he's been through; Connor needs support."

"And I don't?" Phil scoffed. "I'm your best friend, not him."

"Exactly!" Alex draped a rainfly over the tent and secured it. "So, what's your problem?"

Alex was losing patience. He'd grown tired of his best friend's constant anxiety and clinginess the last few days. Knowing Phil was the loudest voice in the room when it came to pointing out the flaws of others and problems but was hesitant when it came to talking about what bothered him upset Alex, especially now. Even as he assembled the complex puzzle that was his pal's personality, Alex felt less and less capable of solving the problem.

"You're never there for me anymore!" Phil's voice cracked. "Anytime I need to talk or anything, you're always helping someone else."

"What're you talking about?" Alex double-checked the tent's edges. "I came to yoga and on the campout. What more do you want?"

"Talking things through would be a start," Phil's shoulders dropped. "Like how I don't feel like I'm good enough for anyone."

"Of course, you are." Alex approached his best friend and patted him on the back. "What makes you think you aren't? It's not the size and weak stuff, is it?"

Alex wasn't sure where all this self-doubt and inadequacy came from. He remembered what his pal told him during cooldowns at yoga about getting picked on by teammates over his size. Not having seen what happened or heard anything about any problems except what Phil told him made it very challenging for Alex to help.

"It's more than that," Phil sighed. "I don't feel like I belong on the team or am worthy enough even to start."

"Get out of here with that, bro?" Alex gave Phil a suspicious look. "You're my right-hand man in everything we do. Even your dad says so."

"No, he doesn't," Phil shook his head. "He was just being polite since you were here."

"No, man." Alex draped an arm around Phil's shoulder and guided him near some trees. "Your dad meant everything on the ride up because it's the truth. You matter more to the team and, most importantly to me, than you think."

Alex consistently heard the expression, "God works in mysterious ways," but never understood it until today. He wasn't sure why the campout was such a huge deal to his buddy. As he saw everything play out from the car ride until now, Alex began unraveling the mystery before him, and it all made sense.

Phil invited me to hang out and work everything out. That's how much he cares about our friendship.

"Do you mean that?" Phil turned to his eyes as his face blushed.

"Absolutely, buddy." Alex smiled. "Don't you think otherwise. You're too great for that."

"Ditto!" Phil draped his arm around Alex's shoulder. "I'm sorry I made you feel like a cruddy person who didn't care."

This acknowledgment from Phil didn't surprise Alex. He realized that his best friend had other kids he hung out with and considered pals, but they were closest. Feeling his heart leap at the fact that he and Phil had worked things out satisfied Alex. It was one of those things for Alex that he and Phil couldn't stay upset with each other for extended periods no matter what happened.

Later, after the sun went down and temperatures dipped to a crisp forty-one degrees, groups of campers settled onto musty tree logs near burning campfires roasting marshmallows on long sticks. The smell of gelatin foam meeting a burning fire permeated the campgrounds and beyond. Chattering people swallowed up the hooting owls and crackles of fires nearby.

While settling on their tree log a considerable distance away from everyone else, Alex and Phil talked through what lay ahead.

"You know we're staying here until Monday, right?" Phil studied his marshmallow beginning to brown. "So, we'll miss school and team workouts."

"That's fine." Alex turned to Phil and smiled. "We needed a break, anyway."

"Agreed," Phil slapped Alex's leg. "At least we'll be back in time for our chapel day."

"Midweek ones are the best." Alex stared at the fire dancing in front of him. "I heard this week is on forgiveness."

Alex looked forward to sitting beside Phil during their chapel day. He knew there were areas where he was inadequate in specific areas, like his buddy, and it only served as opportunities to help each other through things. Agreeing with Phil's mom that God paired them together as lifelong friends for a reason, Alex wouldn't have changed a thing.

Friendship is more about standing by your buddies no matter what and supporting them than anything else.

Chapter Eighteen
Midweek Messages

The Cardinale Chapel was bright and lively early Wednesday morning, differing from the ominous and rainy conditions outside. Stained glass windows with biblical imagery filled the space between white walls. Six rows of cathedral chairs served as seating in the large area to maximize space on either side.

Alex had never attended a service at Beaumont Christian School that wasn't deep and today was no exception. He sat in between Phil to his left and Landon to his right and sang along with classmates during the opening hymn when Bishop Bettencourt entered. Listening to the readings, psalm, and gospel centered around forgiveness, Alex reflected on his late interactions. Then, as Bishop Bettencourt began his sermon, Alex leaned forward with interest.

"As you all may have recognized, today's theme is forgiveness. This process is one of the most important things God commands of us. If we harbor resentment and anger toward others, it hurts us more than others."

Alex couldn't deny that. He admittingly had his fair share of conflicts with others recently. He thought about how reconnecting with Connor only drove a wedge between his friends, leaving him feeling powerless and awful until this past weekend. It had stressed Alex enough that it nearly sabotaged his bond with his best friend, which he salvaged at Bear Mountain.

"That person who may have wronged you most likely doesn't even know they do so," Bishop Bettencourt said, sweeping his eyes over the middle school boys. "You must forgive them anyway as they may not have even gone easy on themselves. It's essential to let yourself off sometimes because carrying those feelings around is a hefty burden."

The first person that came to Alex's mind was his dad and their contentious relationship. He understood his father knew he wronged him and frequently grilled him. Even though he admitted he hated his father sometimes for hardly ever showing up to his games, making time for all his older brothers made weekends complex; Congressional and Senate recesses were especially difficult for Alex. It only twisted the knife further when his dad offered unhelpful criticism and never helpful tips for his soccer development. He sometimes felt that his father's only relation was in name and blood, and they never had a traditional father-son relationship.

That wasn't the only thing Alex considered to be his biggest problem. He had difficulty letting things go, whether it was soccer or the realities regarding his dad. There was one time when he'd played a game of Monopoly with S.J. and lost, which resulted in Alex flipping the game board over and stomping away. After apologizing and admitting that he had acted like a bad sport, Alex had promised to do better.

As Alex continued listening to Bishop Bettencourt talk, he pondered friendships existing and those needing repair. He thought of Connor primarily and how he'd been so focused on getting back to the conference championship than his teammate's troubles. Notwithstanding that Connor had gotten help and was currently counseling with his mom, it didn't change how

Alex felt about not doing more. It was a type of guilt that ripped him to shreds on the insides and tore him apart as a whole, like the way radiation treatment killed cancer cells.

And finally, there were the recent struggles with Phil that Alex fixed only days earlier during their campout. He realized through the argument they'd had that ignoring the needs of his best friend and shoving him aside came with a cost, even if the intentions were noble. Ever since the quarrel while putting up their tent and laying everything out, Alex considered him and Phil closer than ever.

Sometimes it takes a fight or two to appreciate how much friends matter.

"I believe in one God, the father almighty," Bishop Bettencourt began the Nicene Creed.

While moving through the following parts of the service, Alex considered the confession and its meaning. He hadn't loved others as well as he could've. Hearing Bishop Bettencourt saying the absolution reminded Alex that God forgives everyone's sins. As he exchanged the sign of peace with Phil, Landon, and others around him, Alex understood that even if things didn't work out with those he wasn't on good terms with, there was a hope someday that would change.

# #

Kobe Bryant snatched the basketball at the top of the key and launched a twenty-footer. He held his arm in the air and watched as it sailed through the net. Slapping his Los Angeles Laker teammate's low-fives, Kobe backpedaled down the court. Then, leaning forward with his arms extended out to the sides, ready to defend.

"Do you want to watch Halloween movies after we game?" Connor grabbed a handful of Sour Cream and Onion potato chips from a large bag nearby.

"Yeah, man." Alex tapped the buttons on the Xbox 360 controller. "I think my mom is letting us order pizza and stuff tonight."

"That'll be awesome, Alex," Connor turned and smiled. "Is anyone else joining us?"

"No." Alex patted his classmate on the back. "It's just you and me. I didn't invite anyone else."

The two lay on their stomachs at the edge of Alex's full bed late Monday afternoon on Halloween, playing video games on the forty-inch-flat-screen in his bedroom.

Alex paused to observe Boston Celtics point guard Rajon Rando dribbling across the Staples Center half-court and setting up the offense. He wished everyone on the Rams synched like the NBA 2K12 video game players were. Imagining his teammates working together and playing their best gave Alex hope for the Rams to win their final game of the season, a rematch with Greenbriar Day. Knowing a win would secure the second seed in the conference tournament and give Beaumont Christian bragging rights in their rivalry convinced Alex the stakes couldn't be higher.

Ray Allen sprinted to the left corner of the three-point line and caught the ball. He faced off with laker guard Derek Fisher as he pivoted right, then left, and pumped faked for a jump shot. Ray fired a pass toward him after spotting teammate Kevin Garnett crossing into the middle of the key. Garnett dunked the ball in mid-stride, drawing a loud cheer from Celtics fans.

"Not even Phil?" Connor's face expressed a look of surprise. "I thought if you'd invite anyone, it'd be him since you guys are like best buds."

"Yeah, well." Alex stared at the gameplay on the screen. "Ever since Bishop Bettencourt's message on forgiveness earlier, I've wanted to talk things out."

"Ditto," Connor said, his gaze bouncing between Alex and back to the game. "There's something I wanted to tell you."

"You did?" Alex glanced at Connor and studied him. "You haven't had a setback, right?"

Alex feared the worst. He noticed a pattern of late with anyone close to him breaking terrible news or challenges they faced. With everything they'd gone through in the last month, Alex knew that Connor couldn't handle any more adversity. Alex recognized that it shouldn't bother him as much as it did, but it was still a sore subject.

"No, nothing like that," Conor said, pausing the game. "Since I've counseled with your mom, I've never felt better, and I understand what I've gone through."

"That's great!" Alex patted Connor on the shoulder. "I'm thrilled my mom could help."

Alex couldn't remember when Connor seemed so upbeat. He wasn't sure what to do except when he first learned of his mom and former close friend's arrangement. Predicting that the counseling wouldn't have lasted a week and Connor might accuse his mom of bias toward family, Alex admitted he was glad to hear things were going well. But hopeful that he could renew his friendship with Connor, Alex knew he'd have to apologize to him.

"I wanted to apologize for being such a selfish jerk," Connor said, hanging his head. "I didn't know what to do or who I could trust. I hurt you, Nick, Phil, and everyone else on the team."

"It's not your fault." Alex's eyes shined with regret. "It's not like we made things easier or were there when you needed us."

"It wouldn't have mattered," Connor shook his head. "I wasn't in a good place with my parent's divorce and everything. I shut down anyone who tried to help. And you already know what happened that day. I threatened you in Phys Ed and lost it during workouts."

As their conversation continued, Alex traded explanations back and forth with Connor. He remembered a substantial part of his story. Although he'd heard a lot more around school from peers, Alex considered it nothing more than gossip. It wasn't something that he usually subscribed to either. However, Alex understood well how hurtful rumors were.

After hearing each other out, the boys exchanged juvenile jokes they'd heard somewhere.

"Hey Alex, why didn't the zombie go to school?"

"Chasing humans."

"Nope, he felt rotten."

"Yo, Connor. What has hundreds of ears but can't hear a thing?"

"What?"

"A cornfield."

Alex couldn't help but laugh along with Connor. He didn't know if he might join his comrade in the lunchroom again or what the future held. What Alex was sure of was that he and Connor were on their way to repairing their friendship. It wasn't much, but it was a start for Alex, and that's all that mattered.

Alex turned to Connor and stuck his hand out back on his feet. "Friends again?"

Returning the handshake and pulling him into a hug, Connor replied, "Friends."

Chapter Nineteen
Urge for Unity

Kneeling on a rubber mat at the far end of Beaumont Christian School's weight room, Alex raised Phil's leg just above the knee and studied the sour expression stretched across his best friend's face. After a rigorous conditioning session, it was time for stretching, and he paired with one of the kids he trusted more than anyone else. Not surprised by how sore his teammate was since Phil had exited the Greenbriar Day game two days earlier on Saturday afternoon with quad and hip tightness, Alex wasn't sure how either of them made it through today's exercises. It was almost as if Coach Schallhorn wanted to wear them out before this weekend's conference tournament.

But knowing how much the Rams needed to be in the best shape possible, Alex sensed all the preparation their coach planned to help, not hurt them.

The sound of teammates calling out instructions to their companions, Coach Schallhorn switching up movements, and grunting from discomfort attracted Alex's attention. He lowered his teammate's leg to the floor before raising it again. Finding Phil's face buried in his hands now reminded Alex just how strenuous these movements were sometimes.

"I didn't think I'd still be this sore," Phil said, turning his head and curling a lip. "I used the icy hot patches and iced all weekend."

"I know." Alex set his other hand on his teammate's back for balance. "And all the conditioning we did today probably didn't help either."

"Not at all," Phil cracked. "If anything, it only made it worse."

"Probably." Alex nodded. "It's a good thing we're stretching now, then."

Alex gazed at Phil, who guided him, raising his partner's leg further and holding it. The stretch intensified, and Alex heard his teammate grunting through his teeth. No matter how much they paired together for movements, Alex admitted they stunk no matter who was on the receiving end.

"I'm still bummed over the Greenbriar loss." Alex lifted Phil's other leg. "I thought we had them."

"Ditto," Phil folded his arms onto the mat and rested his hands over them. "With the way, you guys played them in the second half and beyond, I figured we at least had a shot."

"Not enough to get the win." Alex pushed on Phil's heels to loosen his teammate's quads now. "It was the best we competed against them all season."

"The best so far, dude," Phil lifted his head and threw a thumbs up. "You took them into double overtime and nearly forced penalty kicks."

This fact brought Alex some comfort, knowing the loss had a silver lining. He recognized that even though their rivals had swept them in regular season play, Greenbriar Day knew they were fortunate. As difficult as it was to walk off under their power without assisting each other, Alex found the Rams could compete against and probably beat any team in their conference. Not one to usually brag, Alex wasn't going to reject his feelings about his team's chances in the tournament.

"No doubt, buddy." Alex smiled. "We'll get them in the championship.

"Speaking of the tournament," Phil adjusted himself into a seated position for a butterfly stretch. "Where are we seeded?"

"Second maybe" Alex shrugged his shoulders. "Which means we'll play multiple games."

"Dang," Phil shook his head. "I was hoping you wouldn't say that."

Although every team's goal in the conference was to secure the number one seed, only the one with the best record had that privilege. He understood his teammate's displeasure, especially with how hard they'd worked recently. Understanding that playing additional games meant even more preparation didn't discourage Alex. He embraced it.

It wasn't long before Coach Schallhorn had partners switch roles which Alex was ready for. He hadn't admitted it to anyone, but he was hurting. No matter how much he did to try and mitigate the aches and pains, Alex knew better than most how much late-season pain lingered.

"No worries." Alex winced as Phil pushed the front of his sneakers forward. "We've got this."

"I know," Phil tucked his chin low. "I hope we last— that's all."

# #

It was hard for Alex to find the right words as he stood in front of the Rams locker room a little later Monday afternoon. He was about to give a speech to his teammates and hear everyone out after. Having a Senator for a dad who spoke on the Senate floor quite often as the minority leader in Washington, public speaking should've come naturally for Alex. But, feeling his heart pounding, he never got this nervous before a big test or even a championship game.

Alex didn't mind talking. He chatted with teammates one by one and in small groups in and out of Coach Schallhorn's presence. Giving oral presentations during class was something Alex got better at the more he practiced. However, player-only meetings led by team captains weren't something Alex considered familiar territory.

"Alright, guys." Alex scanned the eleven other teammates sitting up or standing around. "With the conference tournament coming up this weekend, I wanted to check in."

Alex thought about how the Rams season had gone. So, he was a little surprised this was the first players-only meeting he called. With all the drama early on, Alex figured if the team would've fallen apart and lost their way, it would've been when Connor was dealing with things. But instead, despite all the uncertainty facing the team, Alex found they'd thrived.

"I know we're all still bummed about our loss on Saturday." Alex paid attention to both starters and reserves who contributed to the game. "But we learned something about ourselves and Greenbriar Day. We know we've what it takes to make a serious run in the tournament or win the championship. And the Patriots found out we've got their number."

Alex wasn't looking at things pessimistically. He believed everything he was saying and hoped the team noticed that. Recognizing that it'd be about as challenging as climbing Mount Everest, Alex knew his teammates would be more than capable of handling the challenge.

We can pull this off, whatever it takes.

"Since we just finished up with paired stretching, I wanted to check in with you guys and see how you all felt." Alex swept his eyes over teammates he knew were worse for wear. "We need to be at full strength or as close as possible, so let me know if you guys need anything."

Alex realized he brought up health as much for himself as his teammates. He understood how awful he'd felt throughout the season, and it'd only gotten worse. Knowing that injuries were a part of the game, no matter how much preparation he took before workouts or treatment he received, left Alex unsure how to feel about pain sometimes. At the same time, it bothered him when teammates went down and were hurt.

"Lastly, I just want to give you guys a chance to say anything on your mind or that's bothering you." Alex cleared his throat. "I know how terrible it is when something's on your mind, and you don't feel like anyone's listening. If anyone needs to talk, let me know."

Alex recognized this was perhaps the most crucial part of the players-only meeting. He wanted to avoid future misunderstandings on or off the field after what happened with Connor and Phil. Letting teammates speak their minds and air concerns showed everyone that Alex not only cared about but valued them. Hoping there'd be a greater sense of trust and improved team morale made Alex pray harder.

"Could be better," Landon said, speaking up first and pressing his lips together tightly. "I just found out I'm going back to New York after the semester since my parents finalized their custody."

"Sorry to hear, man." Alex trotted over to his teammate and patted him on the back. "Let me know if you need to talk through anything."

Alex knew his teammate's situation might be temporary. He found out not long after he'd connected with Landon earlier in the season. Stunned at the transformation of this upbeat yet shy kid who also happened to be the grandson of Bishop Bettencourt throughout their season, Alex couldn't have been prouder. Although hearing this news disappointed Alex, he realized it was even harder to accept since Landon's home life was much different than anyone's at school. Despite wanting a championship, Alex wanted to do whatever he could to help and be there for his teammate in the meantime.

"A little anxious," Xavier added. "About all of us holding up for multiple games."

"Agreed." Kellen nodded. "We've got to keep looking out for each other."

Alex couldn't agree more. He was aware of how banged up the team was both mentally and physically.

Knowing that staying united and making sure everyone was at their best was critical for success made Alex's stomach tighten at the mere thought of anything else going wrong.

"My back spasms are improving," Nick said, lying on the floor and pulling his knees toward his chest. "I've worked on it with Vance lately, and X helped me some today."

"Good to hear, Nick." Alex approached his teammate, pressed Nick's knees further, and held them. "Let us know if you need anything or want some help loosening up."

"Thanks, buddy," Nick took a deep breath and exhaled it. "I appreciate that."

Alex assisted for a ten count and stopped. He'd known that the Rams' top forward suffered from spasms since the Seahawk game. Although he understood that there was never a good time for injuries, especially ones that lingered like this one, it concerned Alex. One thing that irritated him was seeing a close friend in pain, teammate or not.

"Nick's right," Alex said. "We're all in this together, and if anyone needs some help, let a teammate know. I've asked you for more help than I would've liked to, so let me know if you guys want my assistance."

Alex heard several more teammates voice their concerns. He wasn't surprised that some kids mentioned everything from self-doubt, academic worries, nervousness, and even worthiness as things that bothered them. Even though the Rams hadn't held any players-only meetings, Alex realized it was a perfect time. Alex undoubtedly recognized how important it was to hear everyone out and see if he could do anything to help.

Chapter Twenty
Flooded with Feedback

Less than two hours later, Monday evening, Alex sat around a circular glass table on the spotless patio of his family's home. He worked on a double cheeseburger fresh off a sizeable modern grill in the corner that overlooked the covered pool. Looking across the table at his dad scrolling through his Blackberry, Alex considered whether he'd listen to what he had to say this time. It seemed to Alex that his dad became less interested as the election loomed closer.

"The most important thing in public office is," Mr. Tomassini said, swallowing a piece of grilled chicken, "making sure you keep the promises made to the people who voted you in."

"Like you did when you served as mayor of Greenbriar." Alex swigged a bottle of water. "I remember everybody around town loved you because of all the jobs you created and how you cut taxes for the middle class."

"Without question, son," Mr. Tomassini said. "Voters want to know their voices matter, and best interests kept in mind with every decision made, regardless of whether you have a D or an R next to your name."

"Sort of like being team captain, right?" Alex turned to his dad and smiled. "Since you have to look out for teammates and lead by example."

Alex understood how important election season was to his dad. He tried listening and supporting him as much as possible and offering suggestions. Unable to get much of a word in about his worries, Alex realized compromise mattered. Not expecting to get much opportunity to talk once his dad's staffers arrived, Alex took what he could get.

"In a way, yes." Mr. Tomassini acknowledged. "But there's so much more to succeeding in politics than leadership and keeping voters happy, and those are givens."

"Yeah, sure, dad." Alex nodded, half-listening to anything his dad said. "We learned about special interests, PACS, and more in Ms. Gentry's class."

"I'm sure you did, Alex," Mr. Tomassini nodded. "You're only getting one perspective, though. It's crucial to hear both sides."

"Right." Alex clicked his tongue. "Can we talk about something else? Maybe the conference tournament this weekend."

Alex had no desire to discuss the logistics of politics right now. He avoided the conversation with his dad if he could, but sometimes that wasn't possible. Hoping to get some encouragement about his team's chances, Alex turned to his dad. Knowing how previous conversations about soccer went, Alex wasn't holding his breath.

"Sure, son." Mr. Tomassini said, setting the blackberry face down on the table. "What's on your mind?"

"I want us to win it all more than anything." Alex raked his fingers through his hair which made him realize he needed a haircut. "Ever since that second Greenbriar game on Saturday, though, I don't know if we can pull it off."

"Why not?" Mr. Tomassini tipped his chin. "From the highlights I saw, you guys had them beat if not for key mistakes down the stretch."

"I know, I know." Alex hung his head. "My passes were off-target, and we missed opportunities."

Alex tried to prepare himself early in the conversation for another potential grilling. He realized there were times throughout the contest when he could've played better. Although his dad hadn't started ripping him apart just yet, Alex knew it was coming in the same way you waited for the great white in the movie Jaws to attack another person every time that ominous John Williams soundtrack hit. With time winding down before the staffers arrived, he waited for the negative feedback.

"No, just the opposite," Mr. Tomassini explained, "you guys needed to stay on the gas pedal instead of letting up when you had them on the defensive. The Patriots capitalized when they saw you all let your guard down."

"Oh, that, yeah." Alex took a deep breath and let it out. "I was expecting you to comment on how we looked tired, and our endurance was awful."

"While all that is true," Mr. Tomassini crossed one leg over the other, "I'd rather give you constructive criticism and something to build off, not tear you apart."

A door opened, separating the kitchen, and the patio opened as S.J. peeked out.

"Hey, dad," S.J. said, his gaze bouncing between his dad and younger brother. "Your staffers are here for the meeting."

"Thank you, S.J." Mr. Tomassini rose but paused. "Let them know I'll be there in a moment."

As Alex stood up and stretched, he struggled to think of a response. He was shocked that his dad offered such helpful advice, given their previous interactions. Mixtures of surprise and disappointment overcame him as Alex considered the timing of his dad's staffer's arrival. A tingling of excitement throughout his body replaced the preplanned feeling of knots in his stomach.

"We'll continue this conversation another time," Mr. Tomassini pulled out a twenty-dollar bill and handed it to Alex. "Have S.J. take you out for a milkshake."

##

Alex didn't have an issue hanging out with S.J. He relished every opportunity. Usually, what irked him was how their dad tossed him like dirty clothes into a laundry hamper during talks, but this time was different. After conversing with his dad, he anticipated it would turn out like others. Alex discovered his dad acted like the father he had always yearned for. After not seeing his dad much, in the stands during the season, and passing him by in the house as if they were strangers, Alex couldn't help but wonder what prompted this sudden change in demeanor.

"I'm shocked dad showed more interest in me tonight." Alex sipped a smores milkshake. "It's great to see he finally cares."

"Absolutely," S.J. turned, then smiled. "You've grown so much as a player and person since the season started. It's not surprising he paid attention to it."

"In what ways?" Alex squinted his hazel green eyes. "Because it seems like all I've done is disappointed dad and ticked off friends."

"We've all disappointed dad, bro," S.J. patted Alex on the back, "at one point or another, it's about picking yourself back up though and playing hard, which you've consistently done. It doesn't go unnoticed by anyone."

The two sat on the flatbed of S.J.'s Ridgeline staring at Beaumont Christian School's soccer field and enjoying milkshakes they'd taken out from Clontz's café. Alex told his older brother they needed to talk after their dad asked them to go out. Not wanting to sit down anywhere, S.J. suggested they drive around and find an empty parking lot.

Although he'd given everything he had on the field since coming back from injury, Alex never considered the possibility that their dad cared about his successes. He found that things only went from bad to worse between them. Even though he wanted so horribly to please their dad and win him over, it left Alex feeling like he won the lottery when he listened to the earlier feedback.

Does S.J. know something I don't know about dad?

"Really?" Alex's shoulders dropped. "I figured everyone expects that."

"For Coach Schallhorn maybe and dad," S.J. shook his Oreo shake. "But to everyone watching in the stands who know what it takes to have success, it matters."

"Speaking of success," Alex swallowed a lump in his throat, "I mentioned to dad that I was worried about our team's chances of winning it all this weekend."

"At the conference tournament?" S.J. pressed his lips together. "What did he say?"

Alex was perplexed by the reactions of his family. First, he swore an alien had replaced his dad during the discussion over soccer that went surprisingly well. And now he was talking things through with his older brother, who always knew the right things to say, yet Alex sensed there was something S.J. knew more than he let on.

"He asked why." Alex swung his legs. "And then offered advice. It was refreshing."

"I'm glad to hear things are better," S.J. drowned the rest of his milkshake. "You know I talked to him, right?"

"No, I didn't." Alex's jaw dropped. "What did you say?"

It seemed to Alex that everything was coming together precisely at the right time. He'd repaired friendships in the last few weeks and even brought the team together during a players-only meeting. Unsure if that had to do with that 'growth' his older brother mentioned at the start of their talk or not, but Alex took it as a win. Even though he didn't want to assume tensions between he and his dad were easing up, Alex could tell something was different.

"I told him straight up that he'd lose you if he didn't start easing up," S.J. explained. "This was a few days after our dinner at Siemian's, where he grilled you again."

"Oh yeah?" Alex's voice cracked. "What did he say?"

"That I was right," S.J. smiled. "Not only did dad agree that he'd ridden you too hard, but he admitted helping you become the best version of yourself would be worth far more than anything he could buy you. And to prove how serious he was, dad said he'd attend the conference tournament."

"So that's why he was being so nice earlier." Alex's face gleamed. "Thanks, S.J. I hope it stays that way."

Alex knew S.J. had his back. He never expected him to talk to their dad in that way and make such a defense. A healthy relationship with their dad where they could speak without fighting was something that Alex believed was only possible in his dreams a few months ago.

We'll see if dad continues to extend support or if he goes back to grilling me.

"Same," S.J. draped an arm around Alex's shoulder now. "What's going on with your friends?"

"Nothing now." Alex sighed. "Phil and I had a rift when we first learned about Connor."

"What happened?" S.J. gazed at his younger brother and raised an eyebrow.

"Phil didn't feel like I was there for him," Alex took the top off his milkshake and chugged it, "when he needed me."

Friendships were meaningful if there was anything his older brother drilled into him more than soccer tips. He went straight to S.J. anytime there were problems relating to not getting along with close friends and situations he was uncertain how to handle. Even as he solved the intricate difficulties that went along with adolescence, Alex felt more materialized, almost just as quickly and further complicated things.

Adults always think life is so easy for us. They have no idea.

"You worked everything out, though, right?" S.J. gave Alex a serious look. "Best buds are hard to find, especially during middle school, don't take that for granted."

"Yup." Alex nodded. "Which is why Phil and I talked through everything during our camping trip."

"Mom mentioned you went there," S.J.'s gaze bounced between the soccer field in front of them and his brother. "You guys had a great time, right?"

"It was a blast!" Alex's face brightened. "I think it was just what we needed to reconnect."

"Sort of like a reminder of how much you mean to each other, right?" S.J. said reassuringly.

Alex agreed with everything S.J. said. Even though he'd repaired the bond with his best friend, it only helped to hear his older brother's take on friendship. Having a friendship like his one with Phil was undoubtedly something Alex would never take for granted again.

Chapter Twenty-One
Pondering the Parallelism

It wasn't hard to drift off into a daydream during eighth-period Language Arts class on Wednesday afternoon; that was at least Alex's view. In listening to Ms. Farnsworth's lecture over their assigned reading from last week, Alex compared Gene returning to school in the winter to recent events involving Phil and his family. A thought suddenly popped into Alex's mind like a lightbulb lighting up above a character's head in cartoon shows as he considered the fight during the campout with his best friend was a turning point in their friendship. He felt as though it was only for the better.

Bringing his focus back to the classroom, Alex found Ms. Farnsworth mentioning the class breaking into small groups for discussion questions. He hoped he got put into his regular group like usual. Even as he credited his teacher with finding questions that weren't only relevant to the material but forced them to think about their own experiences, Alex was left wanting more. Although he claimed Bible class and Film Appreciation as his favorite classes, Alex admitted Language Arts was his third.

While moving his desk with other classmates, Alex smiled, blending with his regular group. He gazed at Gavin, Egan, and Phil, who waited for their discussion questions. Hearing the click-clack of Ms. Farnsworth's heels alerted Alex that his teacher was approaching. Taking the handout and studying it gave Alex the impression that even though most questions revolved around story-based events, others looked for related experiences.

"Let's start with chapter six questions first," Alex said. "How does Winter Session at the beginning of the chapter symbolically introduce the second half of this novel?"

"The seasons changing mirrors the story's mood," Phil rested his arms on his desk. "Everything was relaxed before, even with tensions between Gene and Finny."

"Which shifts after Finny breaks his leg," Gavin confirmed. "And causes a sense of doom on campus with the looming war."

"Not only that," Alex interjected. "But there's an unspoken tension between Gene and his classmates resulting from everything involving Finny."

Alex considered how tensions between him, and Phil helped their friendship. He wasn't sure about things between them leading up to the campout. Knowing Connor's reemergence played a massive role in why they fought left Alex with the impossible task of figuring out how to work things out with him.

It was so much bigger than Connor coming between us. There was no cohesion.

"Compare the Devon and Naguamsett Rivers," Alex crossed one leg over the other as he scanned the handout. "What does each river represent symbolically?"

"The Devon River reflects the way things were," Phil answered. "While Naguamsett depicts the uncertainty of relationships between the boys and their futures."

"Well, that," Gavin said, tipping his chin, "and the change in leadership contrasting Finny's with that of Brinker's."

"Right," Egan's voice cracked. "And Brinker's all about following the rules and righting wrongs."

Hearing his classmate's take on the discussion question made Alex examine the state of his leadership's impact on the team. He pondered if putting winning above all else ultimately hurt his perception among teammates. Even as he considered how he'd refused to get subbed out leading up to his injury a few months earlier, Alex weighed the team's betterment versus personal health.

Would the team have been better off if somebody else was the captain? Or did I do what I thought was best?

"What was significant about Gene and Quackenbush's fight?" Alex glanced at his three other groupmates.

"That Quack perceives Gene as being maimed," Phil leaned forward. "Since only disabled students occupy that role."

"Which Gene takes offense to," Egan said, sweeping the hair out of his eyes, "because he isn't disabled."

"But it has more to do with Finny than anyone," Gavin pointed out. "With Finny injured, Gene struggles with an identity crisis between who he knows and who he tries to emulate."

At that moment, Ms. Farnsworth approached the group's table and smiled.

"That's superb analysis, Mr. Stoddard," Ms. Farnsworth articulated. "Gene tries to escape Finny's shadow to maintain his identity yet loses himself. It's both an internal and external conflict that Gene faces."

Alex gave thought to his own identity with that of his older brother. He recognized that his dad wished that he was more like S.J. in every way, especially related to soccer. Although relationships seemed to be improving on the family end of things, Alex contemplated if he, too, had sometimes lost himself to please his dad.

S.J. and I approach how we play soccer very differently. I used my smaller size and speed to throw defenders off, whereas S.J. took a more aggressive approach. It was undoubtedly a tale of two brothers.

As Alex and his groupmates moved into chapter seven questions, he couldn't get over how real-life situations mirrored those of their novel. He and Phil's experiences paralleled Gene and Finny's, maybe not entirely enough. Although they didn't consider themselves rivals or their animosity between them, Alex knew there was an unmistakable bond between him and his best friend. As much time as they spent together, both bickered or disagreed, but Alex understood neither meant anything by it.

# #

Inside the two gymnasiums, cones were set twenty yards apart for their training session later that afternoon. It was more about keeping everyone limber and zeroed in on their goal. Sneakers squeaked on gleaming hardwood floors, and teammates shouting at each other rang out. A stench of sweat permeated the large area.

Alex lay on his stomach at a cone in the first two lines. He kept his hands in a push-up position and awaited the whistle to start. Out of the few speed and agility drills they'd done so far, this one was by far Alex's least favorite. For him, pushups or even settling into the position reminded him of punishments used by coaches in basketball for failing to meet goals during practice.

"You've got this, Phil." Alex turned to his teammate on the other line. "Stay low and sprint hard."

"Thanks, bud," Phil extended a closed fist out and mimicked an explosion as they bumped fists. "You too, hang in there."

The whistle blew, and both boys sprung to their feet.

Sprinting toward the second cone, Alex remained stunned. He passed the half-court line and felt his heart pounding. Alex raced past the final orange object and braced for impact, rising to his full height. Turning to his side and leading with his shoulder, Alex collided with padded walls hard but remained unfazed.

Jogging to the back of line two, Alex earned numerous high-fives from teammates. He leaned over and touched the front of his sneakers which drew a slight groan. Still sore from their final game of the season and a workout that followed with no improvement, Alex recognized there was no time to let up. Standing back up now and looking around, he saw Nick and Xavier chatting near some bleachers on the right.

"Hey Alex," Landon said, nudging his teammate's shoulder. "Have you seen the tournament schedule yet?"

"Nope." Alex turned and smiled. "How does it look?"

"We earned the second seed," Landon's voice was excited. "So, we'll play Saint Martin's first."

"Solid." Alex nodded. "That's a perfect warmup game."

Alex was satisfied with his team's seeding. He recognized it was the next best thing to having a first-round bye. Not knowing the health of his teammates come Saturday morning concerned Alex. It was a blessing to have a more manageable team to play against first.

It doesn't mean St. Martin's won't bring their A-game.

"True," Landon leaned an arm on the padded wall nearby and raised his leg toward his behind. "We should beat them easily."

"Yup." Alex studied his teammate's movements. "Then we clash with the winner of Montclair Academy or Crestview."

"Dang," Landon winced. "That'll be an intense game."

"Yeah, man." Alex sensed his chest tightening. "Always is."

Alex acknowledged that their team's road to the conference championship wouldn't be without adversity. He remembered just how physical their last game against the Seahawks was. With matchups spread out hours apart, Alex and his team had time to receive treatment, rest, and even scout their eventual opponent—whether Greenbriar Day, Allerton, or Dunleavy. Although he had a feeling that the Patriots were eventually heading to the finals again, Alex was excited and anxious.

Almost without delay, Alex spotted Nick waving and grinning. Trotting over to his teammate and slapping him a high-five, he found Xavier on the floor with a leg raised. Alex's heart pounded, wondering if something was wrong or if the two were just limbering up.

"Sup Al?" Nick said, assisting their teammate with some stretching. "X and I were chatting about the tournament."

"Oh yeah?" Alex leaned over and slapped Xavier a low-five. "What about?"

"Who we'd rather face in the championship?" Xavier grunted through his teeth. "Between the Falcons and Patriots."

"The Patriots, right?" Alex smiled. "That would ultimately burn our rivals when we beat them."

Alex could tell even four days away from the tournament that team morale was high. He'd hoped that his teammates held an optimistic view of their chances. As challenging as the season had been between injuries and everything, Alex couldn't have been prouder of them.

Whether we win or lose this weekend, it was an incredible season.

The whistle blew multiple times, halting the previous drill.

Alex saw Phil jogging over from the padded walls at the north end gymnasium. He checked his best friend's gimpy gait and frowned. Taking it as turning the wrong way during the last exercise made Alex confident enough that his teammate was a bit sore but not hurt.

First, Landon came up in pain earlier, and now Phil.

"Hey, bro." Alex stuck his hand out toward Phil. "You good?"

"No," Phil seized hold of Alex's hand and was helped toward the bleachers. "My legs throb after the last turn."

"I bet." Alex slapped his teammate on the back. "You ran pretty hard."

"Yup," Phil set both hands on his knees as he tried to catch his breath. "Let's work on passing drills together, bud."

Alex noticed that even as much as his teammate tried to brush it off, he was uncomfortable. He looked out for his best friend but stopped short of extending any help before the next exercise. Wanting to see how much either of them could endure without needing to loosen up was Alex's goal for the training session.

Toughness will be a huge deal this weekend. We'd better get ready.

Chapter Twenty-Two
Jovial Journey

The massive, dark-colored coach bus parked outside Finley's Fieldhouse was well-equipped for a long journey on Friday afternoon. On the inside, spacious, cozy charcoal leather seating provided lavish accommodations. Fifteen-inch screen monitors mounted on the back of each seat allowed passengers to view age-appropriate movies. Luggage racks above seats let riders have easy access to their carry-ons.

As Alex tossed his Ram duffel bag into the luggage compartment below the bus and boarded it, this week's events hit him like bricks. He hadn't considered how big of a moment it was for some teammates, especially the reserves who hadn't participated. Traveling out of town to a highly regarded soccer complex and staying in cabins with close friends may have become routine for Alex, but not everyone was that fortunate. This privilege made Alex want to work even fiercer, so his team had a positive experience.

Strolling down the middle of the bus, Alex exchanged low fives with teammates and smiled. He saw Phil slumped in a window seat and planted himself beside his best friend. Hearing heavy metal music coming from his teammate's earphones made Alex wonder if he was upset. Alex's face glowed, elbowing Phil on the shoulder and turning to face him.

"Hey," Alex said, patting his teammate on the shoulder. "You psyched for this weekend?"

"Definitely," Phil turned and smiled. "I'm a little worried about our games, though."

"Ditto." Alex massaged his neck. "How's the quad and everything?"

"Sore as ever," Phil rubbed his upper leg. "But if I get treatment and stretch enough, I'll be as good as gold."

Alex trusted his buddy's opinion. He wasn't sure if the Ram midfielder was worse for wear or not regarding his injuries. His teammate's valiant effort impressed Alex enough to consider Phil a colossal piece of the Rams puzzle despite lingering soreness. As thrilled as he was that his best friend hadn't missed a game all season and complimented him on the field, Alex knew Phil wasn't anywhere near 100%.

"Alright, boys," Coach Schallhorn stood at the front of their bus, even with players continuing to board. "As we head to Kenilworth, I need you all to stay focused and remember what got you here. I'd encourage you all to enjoy the experience and cherish it but don't stay up too late. Lastly, we've got an early game tomorrow against St. Martins, and we'll have another after winning that. Don't take any team lightly. What you experienced during the season is irrelevant."

Alex joined in as the entire bus broke out in chatter and cheers. He was thrilled at his team's level of excitement as they departed. Knowing Coach Schallhorn wasn't the type of coach to wear feelings on his sleeve made Alex's heart leap that their coach praised their efforts. It was one of those rare moments that he would never forget.

The bus pulled out of Finley Fieldhouse's parking lot in less than fifteen minutes and headed toward the interstate. It was an hour-and-a-half ride to Blankenship Bank soccer complex in Kenilworth, Connecticut, which gave kids time to sleep, listen to music, or watch Grown Ups on the monitors.

"Yo Al," Nick said, sitting across the aisle. "Can you imagine if they made a movie like this about us and what ended up like in the future?"

"Yeah!" Alex's face brightened. "It would be incredible."

"Agreed," Nick extended a close fist. "I bet you'll end up a professional sports athlete or general manager of one."

"Maybe, yeah." Alex turned and bumped his friend's fist. "I see you working in public health or some science-related field."

Alex had seen this movie when it first came to theaters two years ago. He went first with his family and again with friends. Claiming the scene where five now grown-ups renting a lake house and trying to relive their childhoods as his favorite left Alex dreaming of the future. To Alex, the movie wasn't so much about the team's success when they won the championship or remembered it but rather the longstanding bond of their friendship.

#

Later that evening, laughter and chatter filled Donohue's dining hall at Blankenship Bank soccer complex. Food set out buffet style at the far end of the room included pre-wrapped sandwiches, salads, water bottles, Gatorades, chip assortments, and desserts. Coaches from all participating teams settled down at their table to discuss how their seasons went. Every squad also had their table to eat at, but it wasn't uncommon for kids to mingle between tables.

Alex took a seat next to Phil and absorbed the scene. He unwrapped a turkey and Swiss on a wheat sandwich and looked around. Spotting his rival and Greenbriar Day midfielder at a table nearby, Alex curled his lip. Having a complicated yet competitive friendship with a former teammate was one of the hardest things for Alex.

"Everything ok, dude?" Phil swigged a water bottle. "You look mad."

"Yeah, man." Alex took a bite of his sandwich. "Spencer's talking trash again."

"Ignore him, Al." Nick grabbed a handful of barbeque chips. "We'll get him back on the field."

"Indeed, Alex," Phil said, curling an arm around his best friend's shoulder. "Don't let it get to you, bud."

Alex considered it normal to trash-talk with opponents. He felt it was as usual as getting taped up by an athletic trainer or going through pre-game warmups. What irked Alex most, though, wasn't the back-and-forth insulting. It was how personally he still took things. If Alex despised anything, it was a reminder to get compared to S.J. and how his teams didn't lose to the Patriots.

"What a cheap shot," Phil almost spit his food out. "Spencer has changed a lot since he transferred to Greenbriar Day."

"No kidding, Phil," Nick shook his head. "He's changed."

"Your right, dude," Phil said. "He's still a jerk, though."

Alex realized his teammate's loyalty to him was like a tropical storm during hurricane season, and it only intensified as it made landfall. He didn't blame Phil for jumping to his defense. Alex recalled an intense interaction with a defender last season where he got slide-tackled hard, and his best friend got in their opponent's face. Considering how fired up Phil got over their rival's actions, Alex wondered if his teammate would remain calm when they faced off against their opponents.

The conversation changed soon after school.

"At least we got out of class early," Egan said. "Anytime early dismissal falls during Farnsworth's class. It's a win."

"True, dude," Phil bumped fists with his teammate. "I can't leave her class fast enough."

"Right." Alex cracked. "The look on Ms. Farnsworth's face when we told her we were leaving early was priceless."

"It was like, how dare you." Phil interlocked his hands around his head and stretched. "You can't leave my class."

Alex stood up and strode toward the buffet table; he couldn't wait for something sweet. He slipped in line and peeked over the kid in front's shoulder to see what was left. Reaching for a double chocolate cookie, Alex hesitated when another hand emerged. Recognizing J.P. standing there and smiling, Alex let his other rival go first.

"Sup Alex?" J.P. gave his longtime nemesis a once over. "Was Spencer talking smack again?"

"Yup. Alex swallowed a lump in his throat. "I swear he gets more obnoxious whenever he opens his mouth."

"Right," J.P. cracked a smile. "Make sure you shut him up once and for all when you guys play."

"Will do," Alex nodded. "It's too bad our teams couldn't meet in the championship."

Alex knew even though the two were captains of rival teams. They'd forged a solid friendship. He'd promised to look out for him on the field and, if possible, suggest tips against opposing teams. It was apparent to Alex, especially now that he and J.P. didn't like their Greenbriar Day counterpart— not in the least.

Even if we've injured the other on a slide tackle or something, we'd both stay until help arrived. That's the true meaning of sportsmanship.

"I know," J.P. sighed in disappointment. "I get stoked when we play each other; our games are epic."

"Agreed," Alex snatched the double chocolate chip cookie he'd waited for. "We play soccer the right way and give it our all."

"That's all it's all about," J.P. slapped Alex. "Best of luck to you this weekend, buddy."

"Ditto," Alex scanned the remaining sweet treats on the table and then turned. "We'll see you on the field, hopefully."

Alex was thrilled to have a positive conversation with an opponent. He knew some of the best and most meaningful games he'd played this season were against Montclair Academy. Having a kid like J.P., who loved and respected the game as much as he did, made it easy for Alex to have more than mutual respect for him.

Chapter Twenty-Three
Doubleheader Dilemma

Within fourteen hours of team dinners, Alex galloped across the center mark of field two at Blankenship Bank Soccer Complex not long after sunrise and felt an opponent crack shoulders with him. Inhaling the chilly, fresh air while he searched for a teammate, Alex imagined his lungs going into a spasm as his upper airways narrowed. Feeling the sun shining on his bare arms thawed him out like a turkey in an oven on Thanksgiving.

He advanced into Cardinal territory, then spotted Phil edging along the left touchlines, and Xavier feinted around his defender. He heard his opponent strain for every breath while simultaneously having his legs kicked. While sending a pass in the direction of Phil, Alex took in the scenery of the tournament; the smell of fresh coffee, bacon, and sausage spreading from the concession stand nearby, accompanied by shouts and cheers from parents echoed from countless Bermuda grass fields.

There's nothing better than conference tournament weekend.

It was a chilly and overcast Saturday morning when Beaumont Christian and St. Martins faced off in the first round of the Pac-7 tournament. The Rams dominated the first half, resulting in a 4-0 lead. Likewise, the majority of the second half was an all-out scoring frenzy in favor of

Beaumont Christian, who increased their winning margin by another three goals. The Rams only looked to run the clock down unless an additional scoring opportunity materialized with less than five minutes to play in regulation.

Although the Rams held a commanding lead, there wasn't one starter on offense who hadn't contributed in some way. Xavier and Nick, the two forwards, each chipped in one goal apiece. The wings on either side, Phil and Landon shelled out another two. And Alex furthered their supremacy with another three goals.

If nothing else, at least this game builds our momentum for the semis.

Alex's heart leaped to look over at field three and see J.P. galloping across the center circle and spinning past defenders before booting a pass to a teammate. He was thrilled for his rival and loved watching him play. Even though he realized that opening rounds for elite teams like Beaumont Christian and Montclair Academy were essentially squash matches, it only forced Alex to enjoy the moment more.

I hope you are ready, pal; we'll see you on the field soon enough.

"Whoo-hoo," A Ram fan shouted, "let's go, Phil."

Alerted back to the action only seconds later, Alex saw his best friend fire a shot. He'd paid close attention to how his teammate delivered that shot from the lift of the leg to the kick itself. Sensing that the pregame warm-up and adrenaline gave the boys even more, boost to contribute to Phil's scoring opportunity made Alex feel better about his buddy's health.

The ball swiveled toward the goal and veered right, and Saint Martin's goalie chased after it as he'd done all morning long and dove. The ball barely grazed the

Cardinal player's extended fingertips and rippled into the right corner net.

The whistle blew, prompting Ram fans to break out in cheers once again and Alex to bolt toward his teammate and seize Phil in a bear hug.

"Perfect goal," Alex spun his best friend around and let him down. "Great job, man."

"Thanks," Phil curled an arm around Alex's shoulder. "Nice pass!"

"Yeah, Al," Nick slapped his teammate a high-five. "We dominated this morning."

"Yup," Xavier joined in and patted his fellow Rams. "Now we have to keep it going!"

At that moment, Alex turned and saw Coach Schallhorn waving them over with a smile. He trotted over to their coach beside his best friend as teammates followed them. While bumping fists with their coach and reserves as they reached the Ram touchline, Alex gazed into the bleachers and caught sight of his family. However, more noteworthy for him was his dad meeting his eye while clapping and nodding his head in approval.

Had he finally won over his dad?

"There you go, boys," Coach Schallhorn said, still clapping and extended high-fives. "Way to set the tone for the rest of the tournament this morning. Now that we're up by eight, I'm pulling starters out. You all played incredibly and earned yourselves a break. For the reserves now, continue churning out the clock...."

As Coach Schallhorn continued talking, Alex's mind drifted off. He felt mixtures of great pride for his and his teammate's performances but was disappointed not to leave the field. Having games scattered throughout the day allowed Alex and others to eat, rehydrate, and recover while ensuring they'd taken care of business on the field.

"Alright, boys," Coach Schallhorn finished his speech and set his hand in the middle as others followed. "One-two-three, Rams!"

"Rams!" the team shouted as the team broke their huddle.

Settling back onto his team's bench and reclining, Alex reviewed his performance. He needed to make better passes and lead teammates in stride to a goal more effectively. Although he'd scored four goals in this matchup, Alex knew the semi-finals called for fiercer kicks.

No matter how great someone plays, they can constantly improve.

This commitment to excellence made Alex view soccer differently than other boys his age. He didn't play and train in any unique way either. Using skills he'd learned from his family and coaches over the years, combined with speed developed through camps and repetitive drills, made Alex the type of player who was a gamechanger.

I never believe or act like I'm better than everyone else. I outwork them.

"Hey buddy," Phil planted himself next to Alex and sighed exhaustively. "I can't believe you scored four goals. That's a record."

"Right," Alex took a cup of water from the student manager and chugged it. "I saw opportunities and took advantage."

"Agreed," Phil leaned back and meshed his hands around his head to catch a breath. "But you also set us up to score as well."

"Yup," Alex turned and smiled. "With the game on the line, you've got to trust your teammates."

On the surface, Alex didn't give much thought to how the words sounded before they'd left his mouth. He'd felt more like team captain and leader at this point than any time during the season. While the team won and stayed on solid ground throughout, Alex hadn't consistently felt that everyone trusted him.

Things were much different then; we weren't all on the same page.

"True," Phil nodded. "Speaking of, there's something I need to tell you."

"Did you get hurt again?" Alex's heartbeat doubled in speed.

"No, nothing like that," Phil hung his head. "I started having these awful nightmares soon after our campout, and I don't know what to do."

"I'm sorry, man," Alex draped an arm around his best friend's shoulder. "Have you told anyone else?"

No sooner had Alex asked his best friend the question did the final whistle blow and conclude the game. He lined up with teammates to shake hands with opponents. As he matched strides with Phil over to the right corner of field two for a post-game talk, Alex mulled over what stressed his teammate so much.

It couldn't be our fight, could it?

Alex dropped to a knee with his teammates, who still strained to breathe and continued dripping with sweat. He kept his arm draped around his best friend, who hung his head and shut his eyes. As he surveyed teammates around him, Alex noticed everyone's eyes were closed and appeared deep in thought.

"Outstanding game, boys," Coach Schallhorn studied the Ram players and grinned. "That's the way to make a statement in the quarterfinals. You played exceptional all game long, but you trusted each other. That's what it's going to take to advance in this tournament. Since we've got a few hours before our next game, I recommend you refuel, rehydrate, and recharge in whatever way you can. Also, make sure you head over to the athletic training center for stretching, retaping, or any treatment you need in the meantime."

While strolling toward the concession stand beside Phil, Alex absorbed the scenery around him. He saw boys of all shapes, sizes, and colors from various teams trot along concrete paths with socks, sandals, or even sneakers. Hearing chattering, laughter, and hip-hop music resonating from PA systems during the pre-and post-games close by reminded Alex of this weekend. The mid-morning smells of burgers, hot dogs, onions, and popcorn would replace breakfast aromas.

"Nope," Phil shook his head. "Not even my parents; you're the only one."

"Geez," Alex patted his teammate on the back. "I'm glad I can be there for you."

"Ditto," Phil curled an arm around Alex's shoulder and pulled him closer. "Remember when you slept over a few years back, and we watched the Scream marathon on TV after trick or treating?"

"Like it was yesterday." Alex's eyes widened. "We ate like half of our candy and three microwave popcorn bags.

Alex had claimed it as one of the best Halloween weekends ever. He had come over to Phil's on Friday afternoon after school. Even though Alex had a blast when they had ordered pizza later that night and had trick-or-treated the next day, he knew nothing had topped watching horror movies on Halloween night.

As the two approached the concession stand and settled in line, Alex and Phil continued rehashing what his best friend considered a huge deal.

"Well, that opening scene gave me nightmares," Phil explained. "And after we fought, that scene haunted me ever since."

"In what way?" Alex studied his teammate.

"Like you were tied up," Phil swallowed a lump in his throat. "And I was on the phone talking to Ghostface."

"I get it now," Alex turned and looked at his best friend. "You felt like you were letting me down or would let me down?"

Having a mom who counseled kids and adolescents for a living helped Alex understand that every kid deals with things differently. He recognized that sometimes stress brings on strange feelings, especially at nighttime. Even though he'd experienced weird nightmares sometimes, Alex knew they weren't real or reflected things that bothered him recently.

Nightmares happen when everything we stress about piles on us at the same time, and we can't deal with it.

#

When Alex struck the ball across the center mark of field two only hours later, his heartbeat doubled in speed. He'd realized how easy his team had it during the quarterfinals and took it for granted. As he hustled into Seahawk territory and felt J.P. crack shoulders with him, two things spiraled around Alex's mind: his dad's thoughts on the semi-finals and Phil's nightmares.

"Let's go, Alex!" J.P. said, his breathing strained. "What do you have left, kid?"

"Wait and see, buddy," Alex extended an arm out and shoved his opponent. "I've got a little something for you."

Staring straight ahead and immediately seeing multiple teammates trying to break free of defenders and cringing at cleats striking his legs, Alex knew he had to get rid of the ball soon.

Gosh, darn it! Would somebody get open already?

"Yo Al," Nick sprinted outside Montclair Academy's goalie box. "Pass it over here!"

"Hey, bro," Phil flashed around nearby. "I've got you on the left."

Alex heard his teammates shrieking but curled his lip. He advanced further and sent a pass in Phil's direction before crumbling over. Coming down on his right side with a thump and cursing the skies, Alex reminded himself it was all part of the game.

I'll need to hit the athletic training center after.

It had been like this the entire game. Nobody had a clear advantage, with the score still deadlocked at zero and both teams having their possessions stall. Almost identical to their prior two matchups, there was no shortage of physicality either, with even more punishing slide tackles, accidental contact, and injuries. There were less than two minutes left in regulation, and boys from both squads weren't giving an inch.

"You, okay?" J.P. stood over him and reached out a hand. "That didn't look good when you went down?"

"Yup," Alex gripped his opponent's hand and got back up. "It hurt like a bee sting."

"Always does," J.P. patted Alex on the back. "Hang in there, pal; you're playing great."

"Ditto!" Alex smiled.

Alex's smile was weak and said a lot more than its author intended. He was playing as best as he could manage, given how he'd felt. Unable to fully express how much he appreciated and respected J.P.'s sportsmanship, Alex admitted how notable his opponent was.

J.P.'s a rare competitor and friend.

Simultaneously, Phil took the ball off his shin guard outside Montclair Academy's penalty box and turned. He advanced and feinted past a defender. As he planted his cleat and fired the ball over to Landon, Phil stumbled over and immediately grabbed hold of his quad.

While catching sight of his best friend going down and trying to follow the action, Alex thought back to the conversation with his teammate earlier. He considered if Phil's fear of getting hurt was what he'd meant by letting him down. Even though he understood that an injury was only one piece of a much larger problem, it worried Alex.

Something's bothering him, and it's not just his leg.

As Alex checked on Phil, his best bud dragged himself to his feet. He studied how the Ram midfielder trailed around with teammates. Turning his attention to another Beaumont Christian player, Landon, who possessed the ball streaking and slashing his way toward the goal, Alex was encouraged until a defender slammed into him.

Come on, man!

At that exact moment, Alex's throat thickened with emotion after hearing a loud yelp before the ball emerged from a pile. He spotted J.P. retrieving the ball and sprinting away. As he raced on an angle to cut his opponent off, Alex recognized he'd been here before and wasn't planning on getting burned again.

Coming into collision with the shifty Seahawk player and sticking to him like flies on roadkill, Alex wanted more than anything to take him down. He noted that teammates on either side hadn't caught up yet, and their opponents had a colossal mismatch. Flying past the center circle with J.P. and advancing into Ram territory forced Alex to wonder if his team would surrender their first goal. He knew Egan had to be getting tired—they all were.

"Let's go defense," Coach Schallhorn called out from the home touchlines. "Make a stop here!"

"Let's go D, let's go D, let's go D!" The Beaumont Christian fans roared.

Hearing the desperate pleas of his coach and their fans, Alex felt a tightening sensation in his chest. He was aware of what he had to do, and it had to happen now. As J.P. approached the Ram penalty box and prepared a pass, Alex lunged forward and stretched a leg out.

Not today, Magliaro!

Alex rammed the Seahawk star and poked the ball free. He crashed to the ground with his opponent, landing on their sides. While deliberating about his huge play possibly sidelining himself and J.P., Alex gazed into the stands and located his dad with an unsettled expression stretched across his face.

I hope dad liked that slide tackle.

"Whoo-hoo, Rams!" the Beaumont Christian fans cheered. "Great save, Egan! That-a-boy!"

Hearing the cheers and lifting his head, Alex studied the Ram goalkeeper's return to his feet with the ball tucked under an arm and grinning. He couldn't have been more thrilled with his teammate. Understanding these moments when having a reliable goalkeeper mattered most left Alex thankful for Egan.

This game has been a goalie's duel, the soccer version of a classic pitching matchup in baseball.

Meanwhile, Egan scanned the field inside the goalie box and moved right. He held the ball in front of him and booted it away.

The ball soared through the grey, overcast skies like a missile before landing a precision strike at the center circle where Ram and Seahawk players awaited its arrival.

Alex used both knees to push himself up. He gazed at the crowd of boys and noticed that Landon, who'd recovered, and Phil were among those competing for possession. Imagining how banged up both boys were left Alex satisfied with his teammate's tenacity and toughness.

"Aww, my calf," J.P. said, writhing in pain nearby.

Turning to find J.P. still down but on his back and drenched in sweat, Alex checked out the Seahawk midfielder and made a sour face. He paid attention to his opponent, pointing to his cleat, and identified it as a cramp. Although torn between supporting his team and assisting his rival with tightness, Alex decided to try and offer a hand.

"Hang in there, pal," Alex knelt beside his opponent's leg and then pushed J.P.'s cleats forward. "You'll be alright soon."

Back at the center circle, Landon smashed into multiple lime green uniforms while heading the ball forward. He tumbled to the ground and landed on his back alongside Seahawk players. As he lay sprawled out with both hands shielding his face, it was unclear if Landon was injured and, if so, how bad.

Alex slapped his opponent's cleat and hustled in the direction of his fallen teammate. He followed the action and then rested a hand on Landon's shoulder. As he checked his teammate out and noticed Landon grimacing in pain, Alex helped ease his teammate into a sitting position.

"You good?" Alex's eyes widened.

"Fine," Landon massaged his lower back. "Just help me up."

"Sure," Alex's heart pounded as he pulled his teammate up from behind, "but you need to see Vance."

"No time," Landon limped ahead. "Go score a goal."

In the same instant, Alex nodded. He observed Phil taking the ball off his cleat and glowed with amazement as his best friend hustled into Seahawk territory, then feinted past a defender. With a man down and time running out, Alex raced on the opposite side of his teammate, who needed a quick cross-pass option. Alex's heart pounded while stealing a quick look at the scoreboard and seeing alarming numbers, a stagnant 0-0 score with nine seconds to play.

"Hey Phil," Xavier emerged nearby. "I'm open, bud!"

"Let's go, Phil," Alex crept along the right touchlines. "I'm over here, man!"

Alex's eyes stayed glued to his teammate, sending a pass across the field before stumbling out of bounds. He gathered the ball off his thigh just outside Montclair Academy's penalty box. As he evaded one defender and another, Alex faked a pass to Nick before firing a shot off.

The ball glided a short distance toward Montclair Academy's goal and veered left. The Seahawk goalkeeper zoomed toward it and leaped in the air. Unfortunately, he was seconds late as it sailed right past the Seahawk boy's fingers.

The whistle blew, and Alex pumped his fist.

"Yes!" Alex screamed. "We're going to the championship.

Alex's heart leaped. He couldn't believe the Rams were going back to the conference championship. As he swept his eyes over his exhausted teammates staggering over to celebrate, Alex couldn't help but ask himself how many of them might not play in the championship. A short while later, he and Phil, who'd finally gotten up, helped each other to the touchlines for Coach Schallhorn's post-game talk.

Looking up toward the bleachers again and seeing his dad nodding his head forced Alex to consider if his efforts this entire weekend would be worth it.

Was that shot good enough, dad?

Chapter Twenty-Four
Analyzing the Aftermath

The nearby shrill of whistles and trash-talking amongst competitors was loud and lively down on field five late Sunday morning. It was early in the first half when Greenbriar Day and Allerton Academy duked it out in the last semi-final matchup. While the score remained tied at 1-1, both teams gave it all despite stalled possessions. There were no signs of either team letting up anytime soon with a lot of game remaining.

"I can't believe we survived, Al," Nick said, chewing on a hot dog. "Montclair Academy gave us everything they had."

"True," Alex swigged a bottle of blue Gatorade. "But we pulled it off."

The two sat on a grassy hill close to the home bleachers reviewing their latest win while checking out the competition. Phil was there too and planted himself next to Alex. Xavier went to the concession stand but hadn't returned yet.

"Yup," Phil raked fingers through his hair. "But not without injuries."

"Right," Nick's eyes widened. "Landon strained his back pretty bad and isn't sure he'll play later."

"I heard," Alex sighed. "That's awful."

"Agreed," Phil smiled. "At least he'll have some war stories for New York."

Yesterday's game had been a thriller from Alex's perspective. At least this year, he wasn't sure how tiresome doubleheader games would be. As he considered the impact of their grueling game with Montclair Academy and his buddy's thoughts, it left Alex perplexed.

Can we hold up against Greenbriar Day?

Turning his attention back to the field, Alex stared intently. He studied the Patriot midfielder sprinting and slashing past countless white jerseys, then lofted a pass to the right. Admitting that he enjoyed playing against rivals, Alex loved watching them on the field even more. Pondering over the possibility that Allerton could upset their opponents intrigued Alex.

"Great save!" the Allerton Academy fans shouted, breathing a sigh of relief as the Falcon goalie deflected a shot out of play.

"Did you see save that save?" Alex eyed the field as he titled ahead. "Allerton's goalie isn't giving up easy."

"Nope," Phil shook his head. "Their entire team is going hard."

"Definitely," Nick drank a bottle of water. "They've got a shot at the championship game, and they shouldn't hold anything back."

"Agreed," Alex sat upright. "I give them credit anyway, especially how Spencer's played."

While limbering up and touching the front of his cleats, Alex contemplated if he needed to revisit the athletic training center. He'd spent about forty-five minutes to an hour after their second game receiving treatment. Although he hadn't sustained any injuries that he was aware of, Alex knew it was in his best interest to stay loose.

The whistle blew.

"Corner kick blue," the referee motioned to the right corner.

As the rest of the first half unfolded and ended with a 1-1 tie, Alex couldn't deny his astonishment. He'd doubled down on thoughts regarding tournament games and their level of difficulty after how different theirs were. Anticipating facing Greenbriar Day for the third time after two losses lit a fire under Alex's behind in a way nothing else would.

For now, though, I'll see how the game plays out.

#

It was midway through the second half when Alex watched Greenbriar Day finally take over the game. He couldn't help but feel impressed with how the duo of Spencer and Trevor asserted dominance over their opponents. Knowing the more energy the Patriot players exerted earlier, the less they'd have later, left Alex with mixed feelings.

We always want to win, but fairness matters too.

Just then, Xavier returned and took a seat between Alex and Nick.

"Sorry I took so long, guys," Xavier said, chugging a cup of ice. "I went to get checked out before hitting the concession stand."

"Dang X," Nick slapped his teammate's shoulder. "You good?"

"My knee was a little sore from our last game," Xavier rubbed the side of his knee. "I'm fine now."

"Good to hear," Phil leaned forward and turned. "You missed a lot."

Alex hated that his teammate felt uncomfortable, even if it was only minimally. Everyone had some minor ache they dealt with. Even though he most likely pulled a muscle or two during the Seahawk game and felt it, Alex certainly wasn't selling anything.

I want to give 100% later, no excuses.

"Yeah," Alex's face gleamed. "Allerton's scored first with Braylon faking out Spencer and firing a shot in."

"Yup," Phil nodded in agreement. "But Greenbriar came right back on a long-range lob from Trevor with an assist from Spencer."

"Indeed, X," Nick flexed his neck from side to side. "Both teams traded the ball back and forth until halftime."

"That's right," Alex draped his arms over his knees. "It's been all Patriots in the second half."

Alex considered how Greenbriar Day's roster was like a group of energizer bunnies. He'd compared their team's rivals since the Patriot players never got winded or seemed that way. Although he knew there'd be a lengthy break for their opponents to eat and recharge, Alex also suspected that come game time, Greenbriar Day would bring it.

Even as the second half wore on and Greenbriar Day maintained their lead, something significant stood out. It wasn't that the Patriots sprinkled a few more goals here or there, but Allerton's defense remained consistently aggressive in the face of adversity. While the Falcons intercepted several passes and caused more turnovers on standout Patriot players, they came up one goal short of tying it up. In the final few minutes of regulation, the Patriots only had to pass to each other to run down the clock.

"Hey, dude," Phil nudged Alex on the shoulder. "Can you help me loosen my quad?"

"Sure thing," Alex twisted his face in concern. Does it hurt?"

"No," Phil settled onto his stomach a few feet away from teammates but looked behind. "Just knotted up."

"Dang," Alex knelt by his best friend's feet and raised a leg. "That happens to my hammy all the time."

Alex never minded helping his teammate. He considered it a ritual of sorts during sports seasons. The timing of it all confused Alex since there was time to head over to the athletic training center if needed, but as he already knew, there was more going on in Phil's head than he was aware of.

Chapter Twenty-Five
Familiar Foes

"Let's go, Rams, let's go," the Beaumont Christian School fans chanted from the away side of the bleachers on field one at Blankenship Bank soccer complex while clapping their hands and stomping their feet. "Let's go, Rams, let's go!"

Alex heard the passionate encouragement as he raced across the center mark and felt Spencer cannon into him. S.J. and their father were somewhere among the chanters like they'd been all weekend long. He gazed to the left and scanned the crowd until he found them. Alex's heart leaped, surprised that his dad hadn't left yet to head back to Washington since Sundays were when he traveled. They were back into the conference title game again, leaving him even more motivated to make his family proud.

Doing his darndest to step up his game, Alex wouldn't let anything stand in the way. He grunted his teeth against the discomfort of his opponent's cleats striking his legs. As he caught sight of several teammates trying to break away from defenders, Alex determined he had to get rid of the ball quickly. The uncertainty of whatever happened next once he passed distressed him.

"Over here, Alex," Phil said, faking left and slashing in his teammate's direction. "I've got your back, dude."

"Let's go, Alex." Landon spun past his opponent and streaked up the right touchline. "Get rid of the dang ball already."

As he sent the ball in his best friend's direction, Alex found himself crashing to the ground. He landed hard on his right side and grimaced. While observing Trevor step in front of the pass only seconds before the Ram midfielder arrived, Alex's stomach twisted in knots. What troubled him more than anything in the present moment was that he couldn't make it to his feet fast enough to stop the Patriot attack.

"Come on, D," the Beaumont Christian fans shouted. "Stop that ball!"

"Score more goals, score more goals," the Greenbriar Day fans countered. "Score more goals!"

At that moment, Trevor darted across the halfway line with Phil hot on his heels. He faked left and cut right before firing a pass to Spencer, who took the ball off his cleat in Ram territory. The Patriot captain pulled the ball into open space and let a shot fly.

The ball soared toward the goal and veered right. Egan hurtled right in the direction of it and dove. In the end, Beaumont Christian's goalkeeper ate grass, unable to stop the goal.

The whistle blew as the Patriot players celebrated.

"You alright?" Phil knelt beside his teammate and eased him on his back. "That was a nasty fall."

"Fine," Alex kneaded his sore legs and disappointedly twisted his face. "I should've made a better pass, though."

"It happens," Phil stretched out a hand toward Alex. "We'll get them back."

"Yup." Alex grabbed hold of Phil's hand and let his best friend help him back up. "Soon, I hope."

While matching strides toward their team's bench, Alex gazed at the scoreboard. He saw that it read, Away, 0, Home, 2, with a little over ten minutes left before intermission. As he gathered around Coach Schallhorn with eight starter teammates, all with large, orange Gatorade bottles, Alex heard labored breathing around him and exhausted expressions. It forced him to wonder if they still had a shot.

"What in the Jim Carrey is going on?" Coach Schallhorn threw his hands up. "You've got to remember what got you here. It's teamwork, unity, looking out for one another. That's what matters. Stop rushing passes, look for better shots, and stop slacking off on defense. Get your heads in the game; you're better than them."

The whistle blew as players from both teams broke their huddles and returned to the field.

That was it. Sore and winded or not, the Rams needed a counter-attack, and they needed it now.

Alex sensed that it wasn't only tight legs that bothered him but an inability to play in a way that pleased his dad. As he jogged beside Phil back to their positions, Alex recognized what he needed to do to get out of his mind.

"Just do your best, buddy," Phil patted his teammate. "Everything will come together."

Alex lined up at his attacking midfield position and waited for the Rams to kickoff. He raced past the center mark as Xavier tapped the ball to Phil and immediately followed by Trevor. Hauling in a quick pass and letting it roll to his feet, Alex spied the opposing right-back straight ahead. Finding himself double teamed by a pair of Patriot players and cleats striking him, he hoped any teammate might emerge.

"Hey, Alex!" Landon called out from nearby as he tried getting his teammate's attention. "Over here, bro, I've got this."

Alex brushed the shoulders of his opponents. He found a brief pocket of open space before booting the ball to his teammate and crumbling. Wondering if the Rams could score before halftime, Alex returned to his feet and surveyed Landon, throbbing back and all, streaking and slashing past opponents. His teammate fired a pass at Nick, who launched a shot toward the goal as he studied him.

The Patriot goalie saw it coming and got a hand up to knock it away from the crease, making Alex's heart pound as he flashed toward the penalty box. Phil had gotten there first, and Alex was about to yell for him to take the shot. Instead, Phil threaded the ball between incoming defenders toward Alex, who was open but would not stay that way for long.

Alex collected the pass and surveyed the situation. He had been in a similar spot dozens of times before. Instinctively, Alex knew what to do, and yet somehow, this time felt different.

Maybe because this was the championship, and everyone was watching. Perhaps it was because he didn't want all the pain and frustration of the entire season to be for nothing. Or that they hadn't beaten Greenbriar Day since S.J. played for the Rams.

Enough.

Alex pressed forward and dribbled around two defenders. He lifted his right leg and swung his cleat toward the ball. Stumbling to the ground and holding his breath as the shot sailed past the Patriot goalie's outstretched hands, Alex peeked at the scoreboard, which showed, Away 1, Home 2, then stretched his arms triumphantly. Hearing the Beaumont Christian fans erupt in a loud cheer and scanning the audience, Alex found his father and older brother smiling and nodding in approval which gave him every reason to smile.

"Dope goal, Alex," Phil said, pulling his best friend to his feet from behind. "Way to score the goal, dude."

"Thanks, man." Alex limped beside Phil as the two returned to their positions. "One more goal and we're tied up before halftime."

I hope dad is proud of how I've played.

Alex paused halfway there and raised his leg toward his chest, then thought, *I'm doing everything I can out here*. Before returning to his position, he turned to Kellen.

"Keep locking these guys down." Alex bumped fists with his teammate. "We've got Greenbriar Day right where we want them."

"Got it, Alex," Kellen nodded. "Don't let up either, buddy."

Bring it on, Spencer.

Alex sneered as the Patriot midfielder hustled around his longtime friend and advanced into Ram territory. He lunged forward and trapped his opponent near the left touchline.

We'll give you everything you can handle.

Pivoting as Phil came over to assist on a double team, Alex reached for his leg after his cleat got caught in some grass. Swinging his leg toward the ball and missing, he landed hard between the touchline and bench.

Not good.

Alex sucked wind. He bounced to his feet and jogged back onto the field, where Kellen and Trevor jockeyed for the ball. Crowding his opponent in hopes of stopping a pass, Alex wondered how many more times he'd get knocked down that day. He hooked his foot's inside around Trevor's but realized the ball was gone.

Spotting Spencer hungrily eyeing the Ram's goal with the ball, Alex made a sour face and thought, *Keep it up, bud, and I'll take you right out of this game.*

He finally knocked the ball free from his rival's foot, bouncing toward the left touchline, where Ram and Patriot players dashed.

There was a brief pileup as both teams tried to keep the ball in play, and they fell to the ground. Spencer was one of the downed Patriots.

It would be easy, Alex realized, to sneak in like he was going for the ball and put his cleats to Spencer's knee.

Spencer probably wouldn't know it was him. But I would know, Alex reasoned. *And I'd have to live with it.*

The whistle had blown to stop play, and Alex sauntered toward the pileup, Spencer still down, and he wondered if someone had stolen his idea.

"You good?" Alex knelt beside his opponent and studied him.

"Hey Alex," Spencer leaned forward to touch the tips of his cleats and held them. "I'm just a little tight. I'll be fine. But, uh, could you push me forward some?"

"Yeah, Spence." Alex pushed on his rival's back briefly and then offered a hand. "Sure, you're ok, man?"

"Of course," Spencer said, taking Alex's hand and letting the Ram captain help him. "All part of the game, right?"

"Right." Alex slapped Spence on the back.

That was close.

Alex trotted around the circle of teammates and opponents, then flashed near the halfway line.

The last thing I need is my family to think I'm a dirty player.

He grinned at Kellen, jarring the ball loose from Trevor and booting it in his direction. Collecting the pass and shielding himself from several defenders before registering Phil racing to the goal, Alex aimed his kick toward his best friend and studied Phil swinging his leg into the ball in mid-air as it zipped past the Patriot goalie into the net.

"Yes!" Alex pumped his fist in the air. "We're back in it."

Alex raced toward his best friend as other teammates joined in to celebrate their team's goal. He slapped Phil a high-five and pulled him into a hug while stealing a look at the scoreboard, which showed a 2-2 tie. Alex could only shake his head by glancing at Mr. Donnelly, the Patriot coach, on the home touchlines with his clipboard surrounded by Greenbriar Day's starters sketching strategy. Noticing their opponent's navy-blue uniforms with red trim, both grass-stained and soaked in sweat, Alex appreciated how intense a matchup it'd been.

It always is, though, he thought. *That's why these games are incredible.*

The Ram players gathered in the left corner area at halftime, where Coach Schallhorn went over first-half statistics, mistakes, and missed opportunities. At the same time, the student manager passed out orange slices and similar colored large sports bottles. Although Coach Schallhorn mentioned numerous big plays, his overall message centered around offensive possessions and needing to pass more to find an open man. However, the coach called for more aggressiveness and double-teamed efforts from midfielders and center backs on the defensive side.

Alex settled a few feet away from the team after their coach's review. He swept his eyes over numerous teammates surrounding them, stretching together, or going to see Vance for retaping or treatment on a training table nearby. As he trotted around and exchanged low-fives and offered encouragement, Alex sensed his legs tightening up.

Just before Alex waved Phil over feet away from the north goalpost, he caught his dad climbing down from the bleachers and turning right with his blackberry glued to his ear. He'd hoped for some advice or feedback, even if it was constructive criticism. Anything would've meant the world. As he considered who his dad could be talking to and if it was important enough to walk away, even if it were only for a few minutes made, Alex was anxious.

Was dad faking his reactions to my games all weekend? Or does he care how I've played for better or worse?

"Hey, buddy," Phil propped his hands on his hips. "Ready to stretch now?

"Yeah," Alex settled onto the grass. "We should while we have the chance, right?"

"Yup," Phil nodded. "If the first half was any preview, it'll only get more intense."

"True," Alex sighed. "I saw my dad leaving the bleachers before; I hope I'm not letting him down."

As Alex raised a leg and let his best friend help loosen him up, he mulled over how much his dad's validation mattered now. He admitted earlier in the season that he yearned for his dad to notice his play and give him some feedback to build off. It was just the opposite, and more of tearing him to pieces than anything made Alex ponder if his dad was putting on a show for the last few weeks or if S.J. meant their father changed his ways.

"How are we still tied with Greenbriar Day?" Phil rested a hand on Alex's shoulder. "We should've beaten them during the first or second overtime."

"No doubt." Alex glanced at Egan inside the goalie box, pulling an arm across his chest. "We outpassed and outshot them."

"For real," Phil said, raising a leg toward his chest. "It seemed like every shot we took, we either got knocked down, or their goalie swatted it away."

"Guys!" Landon gazed at the Ram sideline. "I'm shocked any of us can even stand, much less take penalty shots."

The whistle blew and ended their conversation.

Alex stood next to four other teammates on the left side of the center circle. He surveyed the Greenbriar Day Patriot players setting the ball down and back up three steps. As his mind drifted back to his team's performance following halftime intermission, Alex wondered what went wrong with both teams trading the ball in the early minutes.

Finding his legs barely able to withstand all the racing across the field, assisting on defense and offensive attacks, it didn't surprise Alex that his legs gave out on him near the end of the second half. Having to lie on the grass for several minutes while Vance stretched him out enough to walk toward the Ram bench for rehydration and further treatment wasn't routine. However, it wasn't uncommon as Alex saw boys from both teams suffer the same fate. After everything, he was baffled that anyone on the field endured double overtime and was less than confident about how effective penalty shots might be.

Another moment left Alex holding his breath during a leaping challenge for the ball. He could only look on while Phil challenged multiple navy-blue uniforms at the center circle and came down holding his head which many feared was a concussion. Spotting Trevor exploding past the center mark and heading into the penalty box before flicking the ball toward Spencer, who booted it into the net as time expired in regulation.

Alex didn't believe his teammates were wrong, not in the least. He heard the Greenbriar Day's fans erupt into a loud cheer when Trevor buried the ball into the bottom corner of the net. It seemed to Alex that everything happening throughout the game was fitting, given how both teams had played each other previously.

Nobody expected anything less than everyone's best going into overtime.

"Come on, Landon." Alex clapped his hands. "This shot's all yours, kid."

Alex inspected his teammate jogging up to the ball and lifted his right leg before swinging his cleat into the ball. He thought about how far his teammate had come since joining the team. Unable to think of a better way to end soccer season at Beaumont Christian than making a penalty shot against a top team in the championship game, Alex rooted even more for the kid from New York. Stomping his foot in disappointment, he saw the Patriot goalie deflect the shot.

"Good try, Landon," Alex said, slapping his teammate a low-five when he returned to the line. "You gave it your best shot, man."

If Greenbriar makes the next one, Alex thought, swinging his leg out, Phil *and Nick must make theirs if we expect a shot.*

What happens if it comes down to Spencer and me? We're both great shooters, after all. Would Dad still be proud of me if I blew this opportunity?

Alex looked on as a Patriot forward rifled a shot toward the center of the net, which barely missed Egan's outstretched fingers. He couldn't believe their opponents had made two straight shots already. Determining that the Ram goalkeeper must be hurt, tired, or both, Alex knew it was unlike him not to snatch most balls he saw. Egan was one of the best goalies and catchers throughout the Beaumont Christian School community.

"Let's go, Phil." Alex squatted and folded his hands in prayer. "This goalie doesn't have anything on you."

Alex was impressed with how much power his best friend put into his kick. With the Ram midfielder's quad troubles, he figured that kick would've been brutal. Alex smiled as the ball sailed past Greenbriar Day's goalie's hands into the left corner net, giving the team credit for trying to hang in there on their latest challenge. Observing Phil planting himself on the grass right away and bringing the soles of his cleats together only confirmed to Alex that his best friend mustered through almost any injury.

It'll all be worth it.

Alex passed his eyes over the third Greenbriar shooter, another forward, positioning the ball to take his turn. That's what Coach Schallhorn would say. After playing through numerous injuries this season, including a case of severe cramps at one point, it turned his stomach to see buddies in pain.

Although he bought into the philosophy of winning being everything, Alex didn't fully believe health took a distant second place. Wondering if broken or torn muscles happening, as a result, was enough to convince their coach or even his dad that health mattered wasn't something he wanted to change.

Breathing a sigh of relief when the Ram goalie crawled to his feet and rolled the ball back to the referee, Alex didn't understand how hard Egan landed on that last save. He twisted his face in horror as his teammate snatched the ball in mid-air and crashed to the ground. Whether he was hurt or not, Alex considered the Ram goalkeeper one of the most resilient kids at Beaumont Christian. It didn't matter what sport he participated in with Egan.

A few minutes later, both teams had taken their penalty shots and were down to their final shooters, with the score deadlocked at 4-4. The referee placed the ball down at the penalty marker and backed up five steps.

The whistle blew.

"Let's go, Spence," the Greenbriar Day fans shouted from their feet. "Make that shot, make that shot, make that shot!"

Spence is one of the best shooters in the conference, second behind J.P.

Alex surveyed the Patriot midfielder trotted toward the penalty box and swung his leg. *He seldom, if ever, misses shots*. He thought about how much strength his rival had left as both logged an equal number of minutes. Curling his lip while his opponent jogged toward the penalty marker, lifting his right leg, and sent the shot flying.

The ball flew toward the goal, veered left, collided with the left side of the post, and bounced out of play.

Alex's heart sank. He didn't know whether to cheer this result or console his rival. Experiencing plenty of moments like it throughout his soccer playing days made Alex admit the missed shot never got any easier, whether the first or the last. Despite the Patriots being their most heated rivals, he felt for Spencer, even though they weren't as close as he would've liked.

The referee placed the ball on the penalty marker before blowing the whistle.

"No pressure, dude," Phil patted his best friend's shoulder. It's like any other shot. Just do your best, Alex."

It all comes down to this.

Alex jogged up to the penalty box and swung his leg higher than ever—*I make this, and the championship is ours*. He raced up to the marker and studied the Patriot goalie inside the box. Pondering what direction he should aim the kick; Alex lifted his leg and fired a shot harder than all season.

Please let that be hard enough.

The ball soared past the Patriot goalie and rippled the right side of the net.

"A-L-E-X!" the Beaumont Christian fans stood on their feet as they high-fived and hugged each other. "Alex, Alex, Alex!"

The scoreboard showed: Away, 5, Home, 4.

I did it.

Alex heard the loud cheer from the away bleachers as he sprinted toward his teammates behind the left touchline. He exchanged high-fives and fist bumps. Chest-bumping Phil, Alex thought, *We're finally conference champs!* Lining up with the twelve other teammates for their post-game handshakes didn't sink in that it was the last soccer game in a Beaumont Christian uniform. As high as spirits were and with the anticipation of a Greenbriar Day rematch starting next year, Alex couldn't believe it was over. Losing sight of his family in the crowd, he could only hope they saw that.

Chapter Twenty-Six
Grappling with Greatness

Alex had just exited Humphrey Hall on Tuesday afternoon when his iPhone vibrated. He fished it out from the pocket of his khaki corduroy pants and saw his dad's name flashing on the screen. As he accepted the call and held the phone up to his ear, Alex wasn't sure what to expect.

"Hi, Dad," Alex said, leaning an arm against the brick building. "What's going on?"

"I'm here to pick you and Vincent up," Mr. Tomassini announced. "I hope you haven't made any plans."

"Nope," Alex scratched his head, then twisted his face in confusion. "But dad, I thought…."

"I'll explain everything, son," Mr. Tomassini responded. "See you soon."

It was the strangest thirty seconds ever for Alex. As far as he knew, his dad was supposed to be back in D.C. unless something changed. While trotting over to the parking lot between Sullivan Science and Technology Center and Cardinale Chapel, Alex caught sight of his dad's dark-colored SUV in the pickup line, and his heart leaped.

As Alex climbed into the front passenger seat and strapped his seatbelt on, he turned to his dad, who smiled. He couldn't remember when his dad looked so pleased to see him. Thinking about what sort of surprise his dad had in store left Alex excited.

What could be better than the soccer cake with a trophy on top that he ordered?

"Hey, son," Mr. Tomassini extended a closed fist out. "I took the week off and planned on spending some time with you."

"Yeah, sure," Alex bumped his dad's fist. "But what about Vincent.

"We're dropping him off at a friend's house," Mr. Tomassini assured, "then we'll head over to Siemian's for some food."

"Sounds great, Dad," Alex's face brightened. "But why did you t…."

The back seat passenger door opened and then closed as Vincent planted himself in the seat behind Alex and buckled up.

Alex hesitated to finish his question or say anything else. He heard his little brother starting to tell their dad about his day and drifted off into his thoughts. As he contemplated if he'd finally won the old man over, Alex couldn't help but wonder if there were ulterior motivations for the surprise pickup.

"Sup pal?" Alex turned and stretched out an open palm to Vincent. "Don't forget we're playing the new Jurassic Park game after dinner."

"Yes!" Vincent slapped Alex's hand. "I can't wait."

"Same," Alex smiled. "Everything's been so crazy with soccer and homework, and we haven't gamed together lately."

"Yup," Vincent's shoulders dropped. "And you owe me big time now that your season's over."

Alex turned around and stared out the front windshield as his dad inched the car forward before making a right turn. He heard classic rock music coming from the speakers and peered at the navigation screen. Even as he recognized the familiar notes of Aerosmith's Dream On, Alex imagined that he and his dad were reviewing a film together from a varsity high school soccer game he'd just played in, which brought a smile across Alex's face.

"So, dad," Alex nodded his head in rhythm with the music, "why'd you take the week off? I thought work was like everything for you?"

"It is," Mr. Tomassini rolled the car to a stop at a red light. "But watching your soccer tournament over the weekend reminded me of how much I miss the game and how little I'd seen you, boys, in action the last few years."

"True," Vincent's voice squealed. "Except you've been there in other ways like helping with uniforms and cleats and stuff."

"Yup," Alex swallowed a lump in his throat. "Yet you always show up when it matters."

Even as much as it pained Alex to say those words, he knew it was accurate. He'd cursed the times when their dad wasn't there for him and missed out on important games. While taking note of how much effort their dad made recently left Alex content, it didn't change the contentious relationship they'd had.

I don't hold missing games against him, but it bothers me.

"I try my best," Mr. Tomassini's gaze bounced between the road and Alex. "Even if it doesn't seem like it."

\# \#

The dining room at Siemian's Steakhouse was more crowded than usual at four o'clock. Stressed-out businessmen and single mothers gathered around the bar for early drinks. Waiters took orders from hungry customers and checked on tables recently served. Servers carried out steaming dishes with varieties of smells that permeated.

"You've improved so much since the season started," Mr. Tomassini slurped lobster bisque soup from his spoon. "I mean the way you pass, shoot, defend, and everything."

"Thanks, Dad," Alex said, poking his fork at a grilled chicken salad with fruit and nuts. "That means a lot."

"Of course, kiddo," Mr. Tomassini chugged a large cup of Sprite. "You've earned it."

"What did you think of the tournament?" Alex swallowed his salad. "It's changed a lot since S.J. played."

Alex remembered sitting in those same bleachers four years earlier with his family for S.J.'s tournament. He recalled that the format was double elimination with games allotted for third place. They played even more games, and he considered how harrowing their experience would've been. Alex was thankful for the rule change.

"Very exciting with all the different games," Mr. Tomassini smiled. "Your teams were by far the best, though."

"You think? "Alex's face brightened. "We gave it our all in both quarters and semi-finals."

"And it showed," Mr. Tomassini nodded in agreement. "I honestly thought the Seahawk game was a championship in itself."

Alex couldn't have agreed more. He wasn't sure if he was alone in feeling that way. Even though he wasn't 100% during the conference title matchup, Alex wouldn't have wanted it any other way.

J.P. and I always put on a show.

"Yup," Alex sipped a cup of iced water.

"J.P.'s an incredible player and even nicer kid."

"Sure, seems like it," Mr. Tomassini showed the empty soup bowl to the side. "You two bring out the best in each other."

"Agreed," Alex ran a hand over his sore leg. "It's always a blast but super exhausting when our teams face off."

"Speaking of which," Mr. Tomassini leaned forward and tipped his chin up, "I can't tell you how proud I was with how you hung in there but even more so by your acts of sportsmanship toward your rivals."

There was a brief break in conversation as their waiter approached the table to check if they needed anything.

Alex was glad his efforts throughout the tournament didn't go unnoticed. He'd woken up stiffer than a board on Sunday morning and discovered bruises he didn't think he could get. Although J.P. and Spencer were rivals and pretty darn good athletes, Alex couldn't help aiding them however he could in their time of need.

I don't treat them any different than my friends, opponents or not.

"Yeah, thanks," Alex mustered a half-smile. "I know how difficult it is to play through pain, and if I can help another kid out with that, I will."

"That says a lot about you," Mr. Tomassini folded his hands across the table. "It shows even as great of an athlete as you are. You're an even better kid. People see that."

"It's how you raised us," Alex reminded his dad. "No matter who the best athlete in the family is, our character matters most."

"Absolutely," Mr. Tomassini winked. "And while I still believe S.J. is the top athlete in the family, you aren't far behind, stud."

Alex's heart pounded. Even though he wanted to prove to his dad that he was a premier stud in the family, he never expected to beat out S.J. Recognizing that his older brother was in his own league when it came to sports superiority, Alex was ecstatic to hear he was close.

I'd rather have dad proud of the player and person I am than be the best in the family any day.

Epilogue

When Alex stepped through the front door of Clontz's café, he grinned at the inviting aroma of soup and sandwiches. He heard chattering and laughter of fellow customers drowning out classical music. Out of the corner of his eye, Alex caught several teammates sitting at their usual booth and then waved. Settling next to his best friend, he bumped fists with his surrounding posse.

It was a week before Thanksgiving on Thursday evening. Alex played video games with Vincent almost every day after school, just like he'd promised his little brother. Although thrilled to do right by Vincent, Alex couldn't say no to his classmates who invited him to hang out since they hadn't had much time together since soccer season ended. Making sure to stay loose by jogging or shooting hoops in the driveway of his family's home was prioritized as high by his dad. The conversation switched to early gym sessions as basketball tryouts approached, and he was unsure if he still wanted to play.

"Yo, Al," Nick gulped half of a root beer. "You've looked good during early gym lately."

"Indeed, buddy," Phil said, slurping some New England Clam Chowder from his spoon. "You'll be in the starting lineup for sure."

"You know it, Larson," Gavin joined them now. "You're still playing this season, right? You couldn't wait a few weeks back, bro."

Gavin was around the same size as Nick, with buzzed black hair and friendly green eyes. He was slim like his classmates but had long legs, appearing taller. Although he looked much more fit and fresh than the others since he played AAU basketball, Gavin wasn't immune to injuries either.

"That was before the conference tournament," Alex pulled an arm across his chest. "I'm not 100% yet, guys."

Although soccer season was over, Alex dealt with the costs of their championship run. He wasn't as sure of himself now about moving onto another sport. Unable to hold back the aches and pains during open gym sessions and to have to sub out to stretch or rest on the bleachers disappointed Alex. Recognizing how much of a significant blow it would be for Beaumont Christian basketball, much less his teammates, if he chose not to play made the decision even more challenging.

"I don't think any of us are, Al," Nick said, taking a bite of his grilled cheese sandwich. "I was at the chiropractor's a few times a week for my back until recently."

"Yup," Phil turned and frowned. "My quad's much better, but it tightens up once in a while."

"Exactly, pal," Gavin sipped a mug of hot chocolate, still steaming. "Whatever you're worried about, we've got your back, no worries."

"I know," Alex sighed. "I'm just worried about staying healthy for the entire season."

Alex gazed at his buds, who nodded in acknowledgment. He didn't want to ride the bench, especially not for minor injuries. Because he was the best point guard on the team, much less the whole conference, Alex planned on doing everything he could to stay healthy. After the campaign he'd just finished, he didn't need any reminders about how hard kids fouled in the Pac-7.

"Does anyone know if Snodgrass is trying out?" Gavin interjected. "We could use his defense this season."

"He's not," Phil swept his hair to the side. "Egan mentioned that he and Connor were playing winter baseball."

"I'd heard that too," Nick leaned back and folded his arms. "We've got Xavier and Henry, so we'll be solid."

"Absolutely," Alex smiled. "It should be an incredible season."

As far as Alex was concerned, Connor focused exclusively on baseball. He didn't find a need to try and convince him otherwise. Understanding how much their friendship endured over the last few months made Alex less willing to approach him about another sport.

There's so much more to friendship than just playing team sports together.

#

After three-thirty the following afternoon, Alex filed out of ninth period Language Arts beside Phil. He flipped out his iPhone and checked for missed messages and social media notifications. Seeing a missed call from S.J. reminded Alex of their plans to see a movie today. Without hesitation, sending a text to S.J. that he felt explained everything: I'm going to open gym until 4:30, see you soon.

"Everything good?" Phil turned to Alex and smiled. "I can't wait to get to open gym, bud."

"Same, man." Alex stuffed the phone back into the pockets of his corduroys. "It'll be awesome to play two-on-two against Gavin and Danny again."

"Yup," Phil said, folding his arms against his chest. "Have you handed your physical to Mr. Heflin yet? It's due today."

"Yeah," Alex pushed the side door entrance of Humphrey's Hall open and was met with a burst of frigid air. "I handed it in yesterday."

Matching strides with his best friend as they strolled toward Vitiello Athletic Center, Alex gazed at the tall trees, now bare, swaying from side to side. He knew that winters in Greenbriar started much earlier than in other parts of the country, and it didn't bother him. Pondering if he needed to hit the athletic trainer's room for treatment, Alex weighed how seriously he took pick-up games. He decided against it since Phil, Gavin, or even Danny could help if needed.

Entering the athletic center and crossing through the first two gymnasiums en route, the locker room basketballs bounced, sneakers squeaked on hardwood floors and shouts echoing intrigued Alex. He saw Gavin and a similar-sized boy with wavy light brown hair, who he recognized as Danny shooting around. Tossing his backpack toward a set of bleachers nearby and hustling onto the court, Alex clapped his hands. He didn't care whether he was in school clothes or workout gear; he just wanted to play.

"Hey Gavin," Alex hurried to the top of the key. "Pass it over here, man."

"You've got it," Gavin hurled a pass in his classmate's direction. "Glad you came."

"Ditto," Danny smiled. "It just wouldn't be the same without you and Phil."

"Yup," Alex nodded. "You two ready for that rematch today?"

Alex collected the pass from Gavin before launching a twenty-footer. He loved hearing the swish sound as the ball sailed through the net. Feeling the tingles of excitement in his hands, Alex left his right arm extended.

Being an essential contributor to Beaumont Christian's basketball team made him even more excited for tryouts.

About the Author

Since middle school, William Daye has been an avid reader and writer. As a thirty-year-old lifelong learner whose taken numerous courses in human development, family studies, and psychology, he found these experiences have only strengthened his writing. He's currently finishing his bachelor's degree in interdisciplinary/liberal studies with a concentration in Social Sciences at UNCG with an anticipated graduation date of December 2022 and will eventually become a school counselor.